The Laguna Squeeze

By Jug Brown

ISBN: 978-1-105-12234-7

Available through
www.amazon.com
www.lulu.com

Acknowledgments

I would like to thank Janet Hardy for joyfully editing this manuscript so that it would be readable.

I would like to thank Kim Torgerson for preparing this book for publication and for sending it off into the world with a smile.

Thank you to Gregory Hayes for making a superb cover and for understanding the elements of true absurdity.

PROLOGUE: 20 YEARS AGO

The boy sat on a wall in a park, taking sneaky photos of people with the spy camera concealed in his lunchbox, under a chicken sandwich. He glanced down at the mirror fastened inside the lid that showed him the camera's LCD screen. He framed his shot. His hand moved inside the lunch box to work the zoom and shutter.

Snap. I am watching you, he said to himself.

Snap. A boy passing by on a bike. Snap. Two girls on the swing set. Snap. A woman with a stroller. Nothing interesting was happening today – these pictures would just get filed in his archives.

He picked up his sandwich. Lunch hour was almost over, meaning more middle school hell awaited him.

His best hope was invisibility. Most kids at school never noticed him. Those who did look saw nothing remarkable: a thin, pleasant face, a crooked and shy smile, sandy, carefully combed hair, pressed pants, a golf shirt. He looked like his mother chose all his clothes. She did.

He didn't mind. His bland appearance was perfect cover for eavesdropping and snooping. At twelve, Benny had thousands of candidly snapped photos, movies and sound recordings from all over Eugene, Oregon.

Most of his candid pictures were ordinary. Some were artistic, some really sweet, some embarrassing, some disturbing, and few criminally invasive. Everyone at Jefferson Middle School knew Benny liked photography and cameras. He was the school newspaper photographer and the sports photographer for all the teams. He always had an excellent excuse for having his camera out: he was careful. He had never been caught. He kept his pictures in encrypted files on his computer.

He took a bite of his sandwich, and scanned the park through the viewfinder. Two boys sat together on a park bench fifty feet away – private school geeks, to judge by their uniforms. He knew them slightly. The tall one, Doyle Van Klief, was slouching on the bench, soaking up the late fall sun. Kids called him Dutch. Malcolm Grell, the weird one, was pointing at a book and talking excitedly. Doyle was ignoring him.

"Ms. Cup is going to let me create my own DNA model with nitrogen-based symbols," said Malcolm. "I get to use my own colors. Not like those models you can buy – the colors are all wrong in those. Those models are for children. I know the correct colors."

Malcolm didn't seem to care that Dutch was ignoring him. Malcolm was stoop-shouldered, small for his age, carelessly dressed and groomed.

"It's funny to even have colors with something as small as DNA, isn't it, Doyle? But it's true. There really are colors. I see them," said Malcolm. He hunched over his textbook, jabbering away and gesturing to the bigger boy.

Snap. I am watching you, geek.

Zoom and... snap. He liked both, the close-up and the longer shot. Good composition: One boy gesturing and the other ignoring him, with his eyes closed, kids playing in the background. Perhaps he would touch it up, sharpen the contrast, or even change it into a study in black and white.

Three older kids entered the park. Probably high school kids from Churchill – nobody Benny knew, anyway. One looked Chicano. They all swaggered. They wore low-down baggy pants and t-shirts. They had bandanas in their pockets.

Snap. I watch you, gangstas. He kept taking pictures as the gang-bangers approached the two younger boys and stopped in front of the bench.

"Hey look. It's the lovers," said the Chicano boy. The others looked away.

Snap.

2

"I think they're in love," said the Chicano.

Dutch now had his eyes open, but didn't move. Malcolm stopped talking and hunched tighter over his book.

Snap. Fear and challenge – This was more like it! He sat absolutely still and framed the scene.

"I think they were kissing." The Chicano boy pursed his lips and made a kissing sound.

Snap. The Chicano boy's friends were not rising to the occasion.

"Go away, Victor," said Dutch. He flicked his hand, as if to brush away a fly.

"Fuck you, Dutch," said Victor.

Victor reached down and tried to take Malcolm's book. Malcolm squealed. Dutch stood and pushed Victor in the chest.

Snap. Oh boy, action.

Victor stepped forward and threw a hard punch at Doyle's face. Dutch tried to duck but didn't quite make it. The punch hit Dutch above his eye and he staggered.

Snap. Victor took a boxing stance, both fists raised. Dutch stepped back.

Snap. Victor charged and swung.

Snap. Dutch stepped in close, blocked the punch, hit Victor twice hard in the stomach.

Snap. Gangsta going down.

Victor doubled over. Dutch expertly kicked his feet out from under him. He stood back, breathing hard. He looked at the other boys.

"Croakie, Swede, get him," moaned Victor from the ground. His homeboys didn't move.

Snap. And the winner is…

"Get up, fool," said one boy.

"Let's go, Victor," said the other. Victor staggered to his feet and followed, shaking his head. Dutch unclenched his fists.

Snap. Malcolm clutched his book and rocked, whimpering. Benny zoomed in on his face. Benny recalled all too well his own humiliations at the hands of bullies.

Dutch reached down and touched Malcolm on the shoulder. Malcolm cringed and moved away.

"Time to go back to school, Malcolm," said Dutch softly. "Tell me about Ms. Cup and the DNA model, and the correct colors. I want to hear about it again."

Snap. Benny felt sympathy. His lip quivered with compassion for the strange, terrified boy. What a truly magnificent picture too, so touching, one boy reaching out, the other shrinking back.

Dutch and Malcolm left, Malcolm shuffling, still hunched over, his hand patting his cheek, his eyes darting one way and the other, looking out for more danger.

Benny closed his lunch box and stood up. Damn, he said to himself. That would have been great on video.

CHAPTER 1

LAST MONTH

"Water is perfect," said Malcolm Grell. Doyle "Dutch" Van Klief, straining to hear the soft, monotone voice, caught the Frisbee as it bounced off the cement and tossed it back to Malcolm.

"I can feel every drop of water in my body," said Malcolm. "Each drop is moving around the other elements and enzymes. I feel connected to all water everywhere." Malcolm caught Dutch's toss.

"You're gonna have to yell if you want me to hear you."

"I can feel the water in the reservoir below us." Malcolm's louder voice always reminded Doyle of the atonal wail of a cartoon cat. No wonder he almost never speaks above a library whisper.

"I feel the hydrogen, the oxygen. I feel it inside me. It's just the same as all the water below my feet in storage."

Doyle had heard this a thousand times, every time they came here. Malcolm loved the College Hill Reservoir in Eugene, probably for just this reason: he could feel the molecular energy below his feet. The two had played daily as children in the city park occupying the broad top of the reservoir. Malcolm had felt safe atop so much water, and still did. They came here once or twice a month.

"The nature of water is fascinating. It is gentle, it never insists. It's ready to cling, and just as ready to break apart."

It was great to be outside in the warm sun. It was June, the rainy spring was finally over, and his old friend was talking about one of his favorite subjects. Dutch, who had heard it dozens of times, caught the Frisbee and flipped it back under his leg. He heard birds and lawnmowers and faint music somewhere far off.

Malcolm caught the Frisbee and stopped. He held it by his side.

"I wish I could live here, put a little house on top of this reservoir, on top of this water." This too was a familiar statement. Visiting this place brightened Malcolm's mood every time. Normally his expression was flat and a little sad.

Malcolm's cell phone rang. He pulled it out, glanced at the screen and turned the phone off. Malcolm patted his own cheek with his palm. Dutch knew this motion comforted his friend; Malcolm had learned it from his mom. "What's happening?"

Malcolm didn't answer. He was humming very softly. He began rocking back and forth. His hand was still patting his cheek.

"Malcolm."

Malcolm didn't answer.

"Who was it?"

Malcolm stared. Dutch waited.

"It was him," said Malcolm.

"Who?"

"Cirque du Savant," said Malcolm, his voice almost inaudible.

"Oh no." Dutch took a deep breath and let it out slowly. "I thought he gave up."

"He won't."

"I want to talk to him."

Malcolm handed his phone to Dutch. Dutch dialed the callback combination. Malcolm wandered away.

A man answered brusquely, with a New York honk to his vowels. "Ludlum."

"My name is Doyle Van Klief. I'm a friend of Malcolm Grell, and I'm calling to..."

"Malcolm! Where's Malcolm? I just called Malcolm."

"Mr. Ludlum..."

6

"Put him on the phone. I got business to discuss."

"He doesn't want to talk to you."

"What do you mean? I've talked to him plenty of times. And call me Harold."

"He doesn't want to be in your Cirque du Savant. Stop calling him. He told me to tell you."

"Who are you, his mom? Malcolm's a grown man. I don't have to talk to you."

"I'm his friend. Stop calling or I'm going to get him a lawyer – and a restraining order."

An intake of breath. "Whoa. Where'd that come from? Calm down. Let's just talk. Be reasonable. No need for that."

"Leave him alone."

"OK. OK. I get it. But just listen to me, and hear me out for a minute. If you don't like what I have to offer, I'll never call again. Promise."

"Go away."

"Just let me tell you. Are you concerned about that old bus we used to drive the savants around in? We got rid of that. We're high-class now. Each savant gets his own car now, and his own manager, and his own driver. I can get Malcolm a Cadillac. Nobody else will have a car that nice."

"Go away."

"No more state or county fairs either. All classy venues. Colleges too. Real professors studying the savants – you know – like for science. Respectable. Of course we have to turn a profit, so there's a few gigs with other performers — magicians, a few clowns, dancing girls. Just enough to appeal to a broader audience. Malcolm will love it. It's a great life. Trust me."

"No."

"Let me tell you about the act, uhh, I mean, the other lecturers."

Dutch shook his head.

"We got this one young girl. Eighteen years old and gorgeous, hot hot hot. She sits on a trapeze or hangs from a rope and swings or spins upside down. Totally unafraid. Audience members tell her their date of birth, and she instantly tells them how many days they've lived. She also tells them the day of the week they were born on. Fabulous. She loves it."

"No."

"This other kid plays guitar. Any song he ever heard in his lifetime – even once – he can play back perfectly. Any style, rock to classical. He's still a little rough. He doesn't look too normal. We're working on a costume for him, a big hat, covers his face and hides most of his tics. Very tasteful. He swings in a harness and the audience calls out songs –"

"No."

"Here's what I have in mind for Malcolm. Picture this: Malcolm in a top hat and tails, or we dress him as a swami wearing a turban – your choice. We call him 'The Healer'. He circulates through the audience and sniffs people's breath. He tells them what they ate today and yesterday. He tells them what foods they digest well, and what they should avoid."

Dutch snapped to attention. ""Nobody knows that. Who told you about that?"

"Not important."

"Who told you?"

"What's the big deal?"

"Malcolm's the most private person I know."

"He's a healer. I know what happened when you were kids. Amazing. You're toddlers, playing together, and you stick a fork into an electric socket. Your heart stops. Little three-year-old Malcolm, who's never spoken a word before, calls 911. The paramedics find him doing chest compressions by jumping on your chest, screaming his head off the whole time. They can hardly pull him off. He saved your life."

"Who told you? Someone at the school?"

"I've got sources. I do my research."

"Who was it? Who told you?" Dutch shook his head in frustration.

"Did I mention the pay?..."

"Malcolm doesn't need it. He has a career."

"Career? The Columbia Institute for Research Analysis? You call that a career? If he spends one year with The Cirque du

Savant, I can make him rich. Then I can see that he gets a real career if he wants one. Switzerland, Beijing. Not working for some rinky-dink pseudo–think-tank in Eugene. You're holding him back."

"Go away."

"Look. I'll make you a deal, even though I don't have to talk to you. You go to my website and read the testimonials from the family members of other savants who are working with me. After that, think about my offer. I'll call back in a week. If Malcolm still says no, I'll never bother either of you again. Promise."

"If I look at the website, you'll never call again?" Dutch's eyebrows went up. "Will you call me, not Malcolm?"

"Yes. Scout's honor."

Dutch took a deep breath. Malcolm was far off in a corner, looking up at a tree. "OK. I'll look at your website."

"See? That was easy. We can be friends. There could even be something in it for you, if you know what I mean. Just between us. Nobody has to know."

"Go to hell." Dutch hung up. He walked over to Malcolm and handed him back his phone. "I have to go back to work and prep the bar."

"I have to go back to work too," said Malcolm.

"I'll walk you there."

They started walking down the hill.

"Dutch?"

"Yeah?"

"He won't give up… ever."

"Probably not."

CHAPTER 2

Doyle leaned over the counter at the Nexus Lounge. It was early evening and the crowds hadn't shown up yet. Malcolm, seated as usual at the last seat at the bar, slowly tore open a peanut and sipped a special mixed drink.

"You want another one, Malcolm?"

"No, I'm just fine with this for now. Thanks. I like the sweetness, what's it called?"

"It's something I made just for you. I know you like Coca-Cola but not the fizziness, so I used coke syrup and put a dash of currant vodka in it, plenty of ice, a squeeze of lime and a dash of cold water. I'm glad you like it."

"Alcohol is sometimes relaxing, but I usually don't like the way it tastes." Malcolm spoke in what Doyle thought of as "Malcolm-ese" – a slightly formal, stilted way of speaking that had been part of Malcolm for as long as the two had known each other. "This is good, though. Does it have a name?"

"Not yet. Maybe you and your think-tankers can think of a good one. For now, it'll be 'Malcolm's special'." Dutch placed a fresh napkin and a new bowl of nuts on the bar..

Malcolm left as soon as people started to come in – crowds weren't his style. Thursday was always busy, with people getting ready for the weekend, ready to shed the straitjacket of the work week. Well drinks were cheap and the pour was generous. There were a lot of good seats, live music and fun.

Part of the fun walked out of the bathroom: Benny. Another longtime childhood acquaintance, he had never left town, never explored the world and the possibilities. But he was always busy with his hobby.

"Hey, Benny, what kept you?" Benny was usually punctual as clockwork but it was fully twenty minutes past his usual arrival time.

"I had to move furniture for my mom. I had to finish it or she'd have no place to sleep. Now I couldn't do that, could I?" His eyes widened imploringly.

"I'm glad you're here, it's starting to build and it's just me and Mario. It's a big sports weekend or something. Please check table 12, they just sat down."

"I'm on it."

He trotted to Table 12 and took out his pad. "I'm Benny, good evening. Please let me know your pleasure, sir and madam. Can I start you with a beverage?"

"I want a really light girly drink, something pink and a little sweet. It's Thursday and it's really been a tough week."

"I completely understand. Our bartender can make a dead chicken walk, that's how good he is. And you, sir?"

"I'll have a dark beer, nothing overly hopped like that awful local beer. How about a Guinness?"

"We have Guinness on tap, sir. If you are ready to order, I can put in your drinks and your food or I can be back in a minute. Ready?"

"Well, I'm..."

Benny leaned in close – a bit too close for typical human conversation, nearly licking distance. He inhaled a nose full of her perfume. "It's awfully noisy in here, don't you think? I didn't hear you. Can you say it again?"

"I'll have the Mac 'n' Cheese."

Benny turned equally close to the man, his face only inches away. The man drew back to avoid the possibility of collision. "What will you have, sir?"

"Garlic bread, and the mussels marinara."

"Yes sir. I'll be right back with your drinks."

Benny trotted swiftly to the bar, nodding to locals he knew and noticing that there were four new tables to acknowledge. It was stressful work but he loved the theater of it.

By the time the drinks were in and delivered, the room was nearly full. Benny and his colleague Mario were on the run.

Dutch was alone behind the bar. For him it was a non-stop blur. He traveled from one end of the bar taking orders and overhearing conversations in an absurd collage…

"There were so many people at the campsite that it was like being in a Portland suburb."

"How could he vote that way? It's against all human dignity!"

"He played bass on that one. Then the jam started at about midnight."

"I just can't talk to her anymore, it's like she's just shut down, not listening. I don't know what to do."

"The canned food warehouse has this great wine for $1.99 a bottle, we just bought a whole case. Unbelievable."

"Then you put the chicken in and let it sit there in the sauce on low for about an hour."

"When he came back from college he had a big beard and Martin got upset with him."

"She was really hot that night. We looked at each other but I never asked her name. I am so pissed at myself."

"He had this homegrown stuff that was just terrific. I swear I was up for hours."

"So when someone tells you that a restaurant's 'not bad', it's not a recommendation. They're telling you that you won't get sick from eating there."

"I had to pay $180 for speeding. It was two in the morning; nobody was there but the fuckin' cop."

"Hey, Dutch, whattya got for me?" Dutch froze. He looked up to see Officer Victor Laguna smiling a wolfish smile. Laguna pushed up to the bar between two somewhat anesthetized patrons.

Laguna pulled at both his collars.

He jutted his chin out.

He looked to his left.

He looked to his right.

He leaned in close to Dutch.

12

The Laguna Squeeze. He did it every time he wanted a piece of flesh, a chunk of your soul. He knew you had to give it to him.

"A Ramos Fizz and a Hemingway Daiquiri for table ten," shouted Benny. He saw Laguna leaning in and noticed the pained expression on Dutch's face. He had seen this tableau several times over the last two years. He didn't know exactly what it was about, but he was sure it was nothing good.

"I'll have it for you in two minutes, Benny." Benny and motioned interrogatively with his head toward Laguna. Dutch shook his head.

"Let me get you a drink, Vic. C'mon, it's Thursday. Nothing's gonna happen tonight. How about a Cuba Libre? There's a seat down at the end, I'll get you some peanuts or whatever. You hungry,?"

"I'm an officer of the law, Doyle. Remember, you owe me."

"I remember, I remember, you don't have to remind me all the time. Don't I always come through for you? Give me a break, there's not much happening lately."

Laguna sat down reluctantly. "I'll take the rum and coke, and some fries with a side of bacon."

Dutch nodded and kept moving.

Benny pondered what he had seen but could make nothing of it. No time to think. Must keep serving the customers.

The crowd filled and emptied the seats twice by ten. Laguna had scarfed his food and left. Benny continued full throttle.

"Good evening. Can I help you? Are you hungry tonight or just thirsty?"

"We have about eight people coming and I want a table for us."

"I can help you with that. Give me just a minute." Benny eyed two open tables against the wall. "Stay right here and I'll have you seated in a minute."

Benny put together the two tables and set up the chairs. He waved the man over and in a minute the table was full. It was the Greenwerks crowd.

"The usual roasted potatoes and pitcher of IPA? Or are you guys hungrier?" He noticed a newcomer, a beautiful woman. She stood out like a red rose in a bouquet of white carnations.

"Yeah that's good to start, Benny, let 'er rip." By the time Benny got to the bar to place the order, Dutch had already noticed the new table and the woman.

"I never saw her here before." Dutch bent over the sink to wash beer glasses.

"I'll get her number for you." Benny left before Doyle could object. Every time he looked up from his work, his eyes went to her.

"Here's your pitcher, folks, the taters will be out in just a minute. Anything else you might want?" Benny distributed extra napkins as he spoke. "So what's new at Greenwerks these days?"

"Big rally and demonstration coming up. You'll hear about it pretty soon. We're gonna have a meeting, maybe you should come."

Someone was already flagging Benny from table 3, using an empty pitcher to get his attention. He waved back at them.

"Maybe I should." Benny looked directly at the woman. "But I never saw you here before. I'm Benny, everybody knows me."

"I'm Fawn, I just moved here from Corvallis. I'm running the Greenwerks office. Here's the office number, give me a call, stop by and get involved." Fawn handed Benny her card and shook his hand. Benny smiled and turned. Gee, that was way easier than I thought it would be.

"Here you go, my man: Fawn's phone number." Benny handed Dutch the card.

"Oh man, I ..."

"Just give her a call, you've been making eyes at her all night. Tell her I gave you her number. It's OK, Doyle, she's very friendly."

"Well, thanks, Benny. I don't know what to say."

"Just call her, that's all the thanks I need."

CHAPTER 3

Grey Pearce pushed his reading glasses up on the top of his immaculately cut silver hair. He took a long moment to admire the new flowers in front of the house on Friendly Street. His expensive sandals showed off the deep tan on his legs, and his Hawaiian shirt was cut to highlight his broad shoulders. Incongruously, he carried a briefcase: this attractive little home was Grey's business location, although the only way to know that was to inspect the tiny brass plaque reading "Columbia Institute of Research Analysis" on the front door.

"Hey, look who's here," Merry, the cute blond receptionist, greeted him. "We weren't expecting you till Monday; we were all just about to leave for the weekend. So you couldn't stay away, you had to cut your vacation short?"

"My plane just got in. I was stuck in Mexico City for twelve hours."

"Poor baby. First you had to suffer a two-week vacation on the beach, and then you had to wait in a big bad airport."

"It was hell."

A door opened in the hallway and an athletic young man with a wiry build and short dark hair emerged. He wore sandals and a green t-shirt with the Columbia Institute of Research Analysis logo, a circle with the acronym "CIRA" inside.

CIRA had one client, NanoPharm Pharmaceuticals. CIRA specialized in convincing the public that their ordinary symptoms and bodily conditions – little irritants that they never worried about before – were actual diseases. NanoPharm sometimes developed new drugs to cure these new afflictions. More often, CIRA convinced the public that underperforming

NanoPharm drugs were actually miracle cures for previously unknown diseases.

CIRA test-marketed the drugs and developed advertising strategies. The goal was to make people worry. Grey Pearce and his crew were skilled media manipulators, experts at creating what admen call "FUD" – Fear, Uncertainty and Doubt. They were especially good at selling new diseases to women.

"Grey. What are you doing here?"

"Hi, Lyle. Merry says I couldn't stay away."

"We were just about to leave for the weekend," said Lyle.

"I got a text message from NanoPharm two days ago. They're shipping two new drugs for marketing trials, advertising tests and focus groups."

"That's right, Torpidan and Epithet. They just got here."

"I hurried back. Last year we had no new business in June. This year we have two in the hopper, and three ongoing projects. I think we need a staff meeting today." Grey started walking up the stairs to the conference room. "I want to get ahead of the curve before Monday."

Lyle looked for a moment like he was about to say something. He didn't. He turned back down the hall and knocked on a door.

"Gupta?" An Indian man, busy packing his briefcase, man looked up. "Grey wants a staff meeting."

The man's face fell. "I was more than halfway packed for the weekend."

"Sorry."

Lyle knocked on another door. "Malcolm. Staff meeting please." he closed the door without waiting for an answer. Malcolm preferred as little verbal interaction as possible.

"Staff meeting, Bugs." Lyle left another room.

"Did someone say staph infection?" Bugs called after Lyle. "Do you have staph bugs? Does your hospital have too many staph infections? Reduce your staph with NanoPharm's Ekstaphaless."

One by one, carefully concealing their annoyance at the delay of their weekend plans, the staff of CIRA filed into the conference room. Grey took his place at the head of the table, the place where he looked and felt most at ease. In the picture window behind him, a magnolia tree was in full bloom.

Lyle flopped a pile of files on the table. Gupta sat across from him. Bugs slouched in the chair at the other end of the table, across from Grey. Malcolm stood next to the door. "Bring me up to speed," said Grey.

Lyle opened a folder. "How about Pelucil?"

"Fine," said Grey.

"Tomorrow is the 'Restless Arm Syndrome, 2K Walk to Raise Awareness', the first public disclosure on Pelucil. Then next week we get the name out in the public consciousness. By this time next week our public relations, TV marketing, and focus groups should be well under way."

"I should add," said Gupta, "we are currently approximately 75% completed with the patient trials on Pelucil. The results so far are positive in the eightieth percentile, with a standard deviation of no more than 1.6."

"I'll be there for the run to raise awareness," nodded Grey.

"Good," said Lyle. "I'll be there, too, with Penny and the baby. Bugs is managing the video crew."

Malcolm stood motionless next to the door. He was looking out the window. Nobody asked him if he'd be attending the run; they knew he wouldn't.

"Next," Grey said.

Lyle opened another folder. "Next would be Delaril."

Grey inhaled deeply, and slowly let out his breath. "Any good news?"

"I'm not sure. New findings just came in. I'm not sure if we can do anything with them or not."

"Tell me."

"It has a side effect. Delaril slows down the speech center of the brain. It shows promise for quieting down chattering children, and helping them concentrate. That part works fine, but in a significant minority of patients, this causes the lower lip to droop."

"Only 9.2%," said Gupta. "Maybe within acceptable parameters."

Lyle took his glasses off his head and twirled them in his fingers. "I know about the side effect. That's not new."

"Right," said Lyle. "What's new are the findings from the focus groups. We had a surprising development."

"What?"

Lyle looked at his folder. "Some of the parents with very unruly and noisy kids were not especially concerned with the lip droop. That was a bit surprising. But, when we did single-sex focus groups, the husband group wanted to give it to their wives."

Grey laughed. He looked at Malcolm.

"Is it safe, Malcolm?"

Malcolm ran his tongue over his lips. His hands came up to his face and curled like little paws. He patted his cheek gently with one paw hand. He looked over Grey's head at the tree. "It's safe. I can smell it, I can see how the components fit. Alter one of the amino acid chains and the lip droop goes away." Malcolm left the room. Grey didn't stop him.

Lyle shook his head. "They won't do that. If they changed the formula, it would be a new drug. NanoPharm would have to start from the beginning. That would take years to get the drug back to the marketing stage. "

"Try this slogan! Try Slowdalip!" Bugs interrupted. "Husband not listen to you? Does he say you talk too much? You may suffer from Excess Chatter Syndrome. Try NanoPharm Slowdalip today!"

"We all agree a new name for Delaril is needed," said Grey. "But we'll have to think very carefully about this new application – I'm not saying no – it would have to be marketed perfectly to be sensitive to women. Women are the biggest buying public for NanoPharm's drugs."

"69%," said Gupta.

"How about 'Nofastalip'?" said Bugs.

"No," said Grey.

"Lophosipine?"

"Go back to the drawing board, Bugs."

Grey turned to Lyle. "What about the two new drugs that just came in. What are the deadlines?"

Lyle shrugged. He didn't open a folder.

"The first marketing outline is due in seven months."

Grey breathed in quickly. Then he let it out fast.

"Seven months? Until the first outline is due?"

"Right."

"What am I doing here today?" said Grey.

Lyle shrugged. "I don't know."

"Why did I cut my vacation short?"

"If you'd called me, I'd have told you we have all the time in the world," said Lyle.

Grey shook his head. He put his legal pad in his briefcase. "Meeting adjourned; sorry for keeping you guys. I'm walking down to the Nexus for a drink. Anyone want to join me?"

"AA for me tonight," said Bugs. "No bar for Bugsy." He wagged his finger in the air.

"Wish I could," said Lyle. "Penny has dinner planned."

"Gupta?"

"I must attend my son's Little League game. He is batting only .179. It is not so good."

"He's only eight years old. Give him a break," said Lyle.

"It is true, he is young, but studies show that a student who excels in both academics and sports has a 15% increased chance of getting into the best schools. I am going to hire him a private coach." Gupta left. They heard the front door close.

"I'd say Gupta has only a 15% chance of getting laid tonight," said Bugs.

"With a standard deviation of no more than 1.6%," said Lyle. They all laughed.

Grey stood. "I'll get Malcolm to lock up.." He went downstairs and opened the stockroom door. It was dark. He walked back up. "He's gone."

"He never says goodbye," said Lyle.

"Never say goodbye, my love," sang Bugs, in a country western twang.

"He never shakes hands either," said Lyle.

"Nope," said Grey. "But he's be the most important person here, including me. Plenty of guys could do your jobs or mine, but Malcolm is one of a kind. He's our golden goose."

"Yeah, but he's... weird."

"Do you suffer from progressive weirdness syndrome?" said Bugs. "Ask your doctor..." He trailed off.

"He is an odd duck," said Lyle.

"Duckboy, Duckitis..." echoed Bugs.

Lyle and Grey started down the stairs. "Lock up, Bugs," said Grey.

"Quack!"

CHAPTER 4

Big Art Croakie, the Mayor of Eugene, pulled the Croakie Funeral Homes Cadillac into the circular driveway. Six foot six, one-ninety in high school and hadn't grown an inch, a pound or an IQ point. He leaned on the horn in the same obnoxious way he'd always done, back when he first started using the family business cars as his own: funeral cars, some hearses, and occasionally the van that picked up the messier bodies.

He leaned on the horn again. Karl Olstead, the Swede, poked his head out the front door. The Swede was even taller, at six nine. Both had played varsity basketball and baseball. Both hung onto that memory as if they'd never taken off the uniform. Some twenty years later, they regularly spent hours re-enacting their high school camaraderie.

"How's the big man tonight? Ready for a slam dunk?"

As quiet as always, the Swede smiled impassively and put out his hand for a high five.

"It's our town, baby, we own it and we run it!" Another high five.

Art did all the talking. It was about tonight's event: the music, the chicks, the free food and booze.

The car swung into another driveway ten blocks away. Again the horn intruded loudly. Nik Omentos, another classmate and councilman, sauntered out of his house, unlit cigar plugging his thick-lipped mouth.

Nik's clothes always smelled of food. The successful owner of a six-restaurant chain, he worked continually and ate while he worked. At five-ten, Omentos filled half the car's backseat thoroughly. After ten minutes in the car, his smell permeated everyone else's clothing as well.

"Let's get there early," said Croakie.

"You got a table reserved, what's the worry?" said Nik.

The Swede exhaled, his sole contribution to the conversation.

"Hey, stop the car. I gotta go back inside for a second. I got somethin' for us," said Nik. He returned lugging a 25-pound bag of peanuts in the shell and set it beside him on the floor. He pulled out a knife and slit the top open. Peanuts poured out onto the backseat floor.

The Swede turned and grabbed a handful out of the bag and started to open them, tossing the shells on the floor.

"Peanuts! Peanuts!" everyone but the Swede chanted.

"Wholesale, man, and they're fresh, not like that shit you've been buying at the All-Nite. This is the good stuff, boys, dig in."

Croakie's phone rang. He looked down at it and frowned.

"It's Laguna, I know he's gonna ask about the baseball league again. Always tryin' to get into the club." He shook his head and answered.

"Vic, whatcha up to?... Oh yeah... that sounds nice... well, we're kind of busy tonight... I know, it's about... OK, OK, OK, we'll drive by."

He hit the hang-up button and sighed. "Like I thought, it's about the baseball team thing again. He has a poster, he's right around the corner, so I said we'd swing by and grab it."

Nik groaned. "We got him the job as a cop, an officer, what more does he want? Plus, he gets free food anytime he comes to any of my diners. Let's blow him off."

Croakie yanked the steering wheel unnecessarily hard to the right as he turned up 18th. "You know, in high school he always tried to make me feel guilty for not hanging out with him, as if it was because he's from Mexico. I just didn't want to be around him. He's an asshole. I didn't even know where he was from. Fuckin' Laguna."

The Swede and Nik nodded heavily. Laguna was a perpetual grievance. "I told him to bust these Springfield kids on a DUI. You remember that time? When we had that bet going on the Thurston game? I had to get that pitcher with the

22

killer curve ball off the team. So what does our esteemed Officer Laguna do? He gives the kid a warning and lets him go."

"I remember he came braggin' about it the next day. He got the girlfriend to go down on him or her boyfriend wouldn't be allowed to play. You imagine that? We pay him and he comes back talking about his blow job." Nik shook his head.

The car pulled into the vacant lot on Tyler. Laguna walked toward the car and leaned into the Swede's window. "Take a look at these. I got 'em professionally done." Laguna proudly handed a small stack of flyers to the Swede, who passed them out.

"Looks pretty good, Vic," Croakie pronounced magisterially.

"We need to talk about the teams. I told you about this pitcher I found. He used to be double A. He's from Guatemala, has a 95-mile-per-hour fastball."

Laguna looked around and sensed that none of them were interested in what he had to say. "Wait a minute. I got something else." He strode to his cruiser and came back with a box. "Here you go, a little something for your club house, guys." Proudly, he passed them a brand new toaster.

"Thanks, Vic, but what am I gonna do with a toaster?" Croakie said.

"Don't say I never gave you anything." Vic smiled. "We gotta talk about the line-up for the teams, right? Who's gonna win, right?"

"OK, but we have to do it later. We have somewhere pretty important to be."

"Where you guys goin'? Over the new Wings place?"

"No, we have about four minutes to be at the City Club. We have a special meeting."

"I didn't hear about that," Vic said.

"It's a private deal, invitation only."

"Well, maybe I can go with you. They're not gonna keep out an officer of the law, are they?"

"Sorry Vic, another time, not tonight," said the Swede.

"All right, well, maybe later at the Nexus?"

"Maybe not, Victor," Nik scowled from the back seat.

Croakie began to move the car. Victor stood and watched it pull away.

As he stepped back a cyclist passed on the sidewalk and startled him. Smoothly, Laguna threw his hip into the rider. "Hey, watch where you're going, dickhead!" he snarled as the kid hit the ground.

"I saw that! You saw me coming, you did that on purpose!"

Laguna reached down and grabbed the kid's hand and pulled him up. "Now that's just silly talk, isn't it?" He glared into the kid's face and squeezed his hand, hard. "You didn't see any such thing, son."

The kid turned his face away angrily and reached down to pick up his bike. Both he and Laguna saw the broken taillight.

"Now, this isn't something you want to tell your mom about, you know. She'll just think you're bein' careless. Maybe you shouldn't be allowed to ride your bike, if you're gonna be havin' accidents and breakin' it."

Laguna stepped closer and put his foot onto a colorful streamer coming from the bike handle, preventing the boy from reclaiming his property. "Don't be so sad, son. The wheels haven't bent and all the spokes are still there. Now I suggest you go right home."

Laguna turned and the kid left silently.

CHAPTER 5

"There are six trees to protect from the chainsaws tomorrow, and 23 of us want to be in those trees. So we're gonna choose six people at random. Write your name down and put it into the hat," said Macrouder, the founder of Greenwerks. He dropped a slip of paper into the hat and passed the hat on.

"This is the last chance to say goodbye to those ancient trees. I doubt we'll save them. But tomorrow we say no to the developers. We say no to the corporate vampires, and we say no to Mayor Croakie. We also say no to anyone who still believes that the system might be fixable. Tomorrow we say no, no, no."

Macrouder looked out over a few dozen hippies, college students, runaways and dropouts, all nodding emphatically. He recognized only a few. Different people, same costumes, he thought. People joined and left Greenwerks frequently. The new faces made him realize that he would need to explain the principles of non-violent resistance one more time. He didn't mind. Some rules were worth following.

Greenwerks was a loose-knit organization dedicated to radical recycling, non-violent resistance, alternative energy and a low-carbon-footprint lifestyle. They took to the streets often. Macrouder had founded the group two years before, with a grant he applied for during his senior year at the University of Oregon. He used the money to rent a single large room above a Chinese restaurant on Willamette Street next to the train station. He wrote the bylaws, then put out the word on the Internet, in the classrooms and on the street. The only furniture in the office was folding chairs and a couple of tables covered with laptops, leaflets and food wrappers. Sometimes homeless teens slept there.

Macrouder was 33 years old, dressed in a t-shirt and shorts, medium tall and scrawny. He had a scant goatee and mustache and some halfhearted sideburns. His dark hair wasn't long, but always looked uncombed. One ear was pierced. His smile was friendly, but his dark eyes held a tired and questioning expression.

Macrouder considered himself an organizer, not a leader. He trained others how to organize. Wherever possible he stepped back, encouraging people to split off from the main group, form their own groups, and make their own rules. He considered himself a full-time, non-violent revolutionary.

He watched as six names, none his, were chosen. That meant tomorrow he would be on the ground, in the crowd, chanting and resisting the City's plan to cut six old-growth maple trees and build cheap condominiums off the downtown mall.

The room was now buzzing, as the six tree sitters became mini-celebrities for the evening. It was time.

"Resistance is holy," Macrouder said loudly.

The buzz continued at full volume.

"Resistance is holy, all by itself."

The buzz muted.

"We resist. It's all we have left."

The room was quiet.

"Some well-meaning people tell me: Reform from the inside, seek incremental change. Use compromise, save the system. Those people are wrong. Compromise will fail. The power imbalance is now too great. There is no hope for reform by trying to take the mechanisms of power away from the corporate elite, and there's no point in trying. They have the money, they have the media, they have the US fucking Supreme Court, and they control how the government is chosen."

Macrouder began to pace. "We lost. We can't change it from the inside. The only good news is that capitalism is dying by its own hand. America is over. The early signs are everywhere. As it goes down, we wonder: Will totalitarian capitalism destroy our ecosystem in its death throes? Will the big event that finally topples it be an economic collapse or an ecological one? How many more millions will suffer?"

He had their attention.

"They keep us distracted and off-balance with celebrity gossip and promises that we too can be rich and beautiful – just like the elite. They want us to be self-absorbed, dazed and confused. They want us passively playing with our electronic toys like kittens playing with shiny objects dangling from a string. They want to divide us from each other by mobilizing hatred, and by denigrating the idea of helping the unfortunate. If you aren't rich, it's your own fault. Hey! Oprah made it big, so why not you?"

He stopped pacing and focused on the audience, one pair of eyes at the time. "Why get up into those trees? It's pointless, right?" He nodded his head. Eyes widened. "Sure it is. It's absurd. You won't save those trees. They'll cut them tomorrow, and you will be torn out of those trees, and then you'll be made into the villain. I guarantee it. You will be arrested, at least. You might get clubbed. You might get gassed. You might fall down from the tree and break your neck and end up in a wheelchair."

He stopped pacing and looked at his listeners, making intense eye contact with them one by one. "So... why do we get into those trees?"

"Because the trees are important?" said a young woman in black Goth clothes.

"Yes. Sure. But let's look at the big picture. Albert Camus, the philosopher, wrote that life is meaningless. We are alone, we suffer, we die – the end." He laughed. "That's a pretty bleak viewpoint."

He shrugged. "However, he also believed that resistance, even futile resistance, is the only worthwhile response to an absurd, violent world designed to enrich the few at the expense of the many. He believed in resistance for its own sake."

27

Macrouder took a deep breath. "Resistance, simple resistance for its own sake, anytime and anyplace, is the only way to be an authentic human being in a bleak, absurd world, in a world of organized corporate crime, human degradation and environmental collapse."

Figuring he'd done the angry stuff long enough, Macrouder allowed his naturally lovely smile to emerge. He spread his hands wide. "Resistance is beautiful. Resistance affirms life. Resistance is faith. Resistance is spiritual. To defy is to be truly alive and meaningful. As long as we defy, our children will have a chance, however small. Our puny resistance now is a light into the future."

"Yeah. Kill the motherfuckers," shouted a new boy, a street kid with a backpack.

Macrouder held up his hands. "Let's look at violence. The corporate system glorifies it. Corporations profit by it. Do you want to become like the corporations? Health insurance companies make money by denying benefits and causing death. Mining companies blow the tops off mountains and poison the people downstream."

He shook his head. "Violence is a drug. The corporate vampires and their enablers like Mayor Croakie are addicted to it. They are indifferent to suffering. They want us to be like them – or shut up and go away. They want to keep us apart from each other. They want to prevent us from caring for the unfortunate and the environment. If we use violence, they'll call us as terrorists. They'll sell that image to the world using their overwhelming media control. That label will justify harsh measures."

He looked directly at the street kid who'd spoken up. "No. We are strictly non-violent. Yes, we actively resist, but we don't damage property or hurt people."

Macrouder stood still and waited a long moment. "If anybody here wants to fight the police, or break windows, or start fires, don't come tomorrow. Stay home. I'm serious."

Nobody said anything.

He smiled.

"Good. I'm proud of you. At 3:00 a.m., we meet at the trees. Tomorrow we say... No!"

"No! No! No!" the crowd echoed.

CHAPTER 6

Grey Pearce and Lyle Vannet both arrived early at the South Eugene High School parking lot. It was the day of the Walk to Raise Awareness about Restless Arm Syndrome. Bugs Grainger showed up soon after with the camera crew. The air was warm and the day promised to be sunny and breezy.

Grey had high hopes for a lot of great publicity for Restless Arm Syndrome. This was NanoPharm's first public exposure for Pelucil. After today, The Columbia Institute for Research Analysis would test television ads, start patient trials, and begin a series of focus groups, their goal to find out if restless arm syndrome would catch on with the public. They would recognize success when people in Eugene asked their doctors for Pelucil, NanoPharm's wonder drug. If that went well, NanoPharm would go national with Pelucil. Eugene, with its mix of highly educated and blue-collar people, was ideal for test-marketing new drugs.

As the starting time approached, Grey's hopes for a big turnout dwindled. Very few runners showed up, despite an advertising blitz in the last two weeks. When the walk began, they had 25 people, including six Girl Scouts in uniform, a few parents with strollers, and the CIRA staff and families.

"Less than a one-hundredth of one percent turnout per advertising dollar," said Gupta, lacing up his shoes.

"I have five good camera spots, Grey," said Bugs. "Don't worry. I can make this march look huge. Just don't bunch together. Stay apart."

"Did you hear about the trees?" said Lyle.

"What trees?" said Grey, crankily.

"Our race ends near a new construction site downtown. There have been arguments between pro-development and anti-development factions for weeks about some historic trees. Construction starts today, and the trees are coming down."

"Good. Let's go watch them cut down the damn trees," muttered Grey.

A couple of Girl Scouts overheard him. One looked like she might cry. Grey smiled at her.

Lyle shot Grey a disapproving look, and stepped over to defuse the situation. He took the girls aside and gave each one the corner of the sign. It said "NanoPharm. Searching for a Cure – Restless Arm Syndrome." This seemed to cheer them up.

Grey turned to the small gathering.

"Let's march for a cure. Have fun!"

CHAPTER 7

At first daylight, Fawn Fallingsnow had started videotaping the tree-sitters for Greenwerks. She had plenty of videotape and fresh batteries. She stood on a milk crate next to a dumpster across the street. Even though she was only five-two, she had a good view of the six old trees. If necessary, she could climb on the dumpster.

She shot some film of LeBron Booker up in his tree. He waved his bullhorn at her. LeBron was the son of a Bay Area jazz bassist father and a radical Jewish leftist mother. He had tied himself high up in the biggest maple tree. Like everyone in the trees, he was wearing goggles and a bandana in case of tear gas.

The Greenwerks banner – Action Now! – stretched between LeBron and Tara Keithers. An experienced rock climber, Tara sat easily on a branch. Both activists were tied to climbing ropes. The other four tree-sitters were less experienced. They sat lower in their trees, ready for a safe exit.

As they waited, the tree-sitters sent streams of text messages, photos and tweets to thousands of environmental sympathizers all over the Pacific Northwest. Early-morning risers on their lists tweeted back to them. Some promised to hurry down and join the protest.

At 8 a.m., the tree cutting crew arrived. They saw the tree-sitters and the protesters surrounding each tree, inside the chain link fence.

The crew boss ordered the protesters off. The protesters chanted, in the manner of protesters for decades, "Hell no, we won't go!"

The crew boss threatened to call the police. The protesters chanted, "Save the trees, save the trees."

"Fuckin' hippies. You fuckin' scum," the crew boss cursed.

"Join us, join us," the protesters chanted.

The crew boss called the police. The police called Mayor Art Croakie. Croakie sat up in bed and ordered the police and all reserves to the scene. He kissed Beatrice, who was sleeping soundly under the influence of sleeping pills. Croakie put on a light grey suit, a freshly pressed shirt, and a red, white and blue tie. He was camera-ready as he opened the door of his Cadillac. He swept the peanut shells off the seat with his hand and backed out of his garage.

When Croakie arrived at the protest site, the crowd was growing and the police were milling around. He parked across the street, in front of a dumpster. He noticed a hippie girl with a video camera standing on a box, but dismissed her as harmless.

The police and protesters were in separate groups, the police glaring, the protesters chanting. In the trees, LeBron and Tara were standing on their branches, leading the chants with bullhorns.

The three local networks arrived. They set up TV cameras next to uplink trucks.

The Eugene police chief came up to the Caddy and handed Croakie a hand-held radio.

"What a fuckin' mess," said the Chief, leaning on the car. He grabbed a handful of peanuts.

"What are we waiting for?" said Croakie. "Clear 'em out."

"We're waiting for the boom truck and bucket."

"Jesus Christ," said Croakie. "At least get rid of the protesters surrounding the trees. They're trespassing."

"Your call. I'll be listening." The Chief walked off.

New protesters arrived and joined the throng near the fence, streaming in from all sides.

"Get a move on, Chief," said Croakie into the walkie-talkie. "Is that Officer Laguna?"

"He's here," the radio crackled.

"Send him up in the cherry-picker when it gets here. He'll kick ass."

"Roger," said the Chief.

The construction workers removed the fence and stood back. The protesters sat with their backs to the trees, their arms linked.

"We order you to leave now. You are trespassing. Leave the trees now, or you will be arrested," shouted the chief, his voice magnified by his bullhorn.

"Hell no, we won't go," answered LeBron, even louder. The crowd took up the chant. "Hell no, we won't go."

The police wore riot helmets and held shields and batons. The Chief nodded to six officers, including Laguna. They put down their shields and charged. Victor Laguna was in front. He rammed his baton into the stomach of a boy. The boy doubled over. The boys next to him tried to hold on to his arms. Laguna bashed them on the arms. They screamed and let go.

The police swarmed in. To Croakie, they looked like a feeding frenzy from Animal Planet. Big Art felt a big erection growing. Down, linebacker, he said to it, using his pet name. Down, boy.

Fawn Fallingsnow climbed up on the dumpster. She had a perfect view from above the melee. She filmed the charge. She filmed Laguna striking the protesters. The charging police looked to her like a swarm of killer bees. The TV crews filmed the charge.

Grey Pearce and his marchers heard the chanting and the bullhorns several blocks before they arrived at the protest. It sounded exciting, so they hurried to get there.

Grey caught up to Lyle. "Maybe there are TV cameras? Can we get the Restless Arm Syndrome banner in front of the TV cameras, do you think? That would be worth thousands in free advertising if they show our banner on the news."

"Good idea. Great idea," said Lyle.

They arrived at the outskirts of the growing mob. Most people in the large crowd were just curious onlookers. Hardcore protesters moved toward the action. The police with shields now had their backs to the trees, facing the mass of new protesters. Behind the wall of shields, Laguna and others dragged limp handcuffed protesters, away from the trees. The protesters went limp. The police hauled them to a jail bus.

Grey surveyed the packed crowd. It looked impossible to get through. He gathered the remainder of his runners and walkers across the street. The bullhorns made it difficult to hear, so he shouted. Two Girl Scouts still held up the Restless Arm Syndrome banner between them. Grey squatted down next to them.

"Do you want to be on TV? Like reality TV?" he asked the two girls.

"Yeah!" They grinned excitedly.

"Good. Just follow me. This will be fun. You're gonna to be on TV!" Grey took one girl by the hand and started pushing and shoving his way through the crowd, towards the TV cameras.

Croakie called the Chief. "Get Laguna in that bucket. Get him up there." He pushed the button for the Swede.

"You gotta see this. I'm down at the fucking trees. The protesters are all over them, makin' noise, sounds like a bunch of apes. The police are about to bust their fuzzy heads... uh, gotta go." The Chief needed his attention.

"Laguna's in the bucket," said the Chief.

"Send him up. Do it. Teach 'em a lesson."

Croakie ate some peanuts and tossed the shells on the ground. What a show.

The police pushed the crowd back with their shields to make way for the boom truck. The boom truck moved to the first tree, where Tara was roped. As the cop-carrying bucket rose to her, Tara kept chanting. The other tree-sitters shouted encouragement. LeBron went on shouting, bullhorn-amplified, "Save the trees. Save the trees. Stop the developers." The crowd chanted with him.

"Get in the bucket," Laguna ordered Tara. He held a can of pepper spray. Wide-eyed, she caved. Her protest moment was over. She reached out her hand and Laguna snapped a cuff on and tightened it painfully hard. He reached over and plucked her off the branch, grabbing her by the crotch to hoist her into the bucket. He turned her around and finished cuffing her, his crotch pressed hard against her ass.

Fawn Fallingsnow had a perfect view. She videotaped the handcuffing, the crotch grabbing and the ass grinding.

The TV cameras also had a perfect view. They videotaped it all.

Bugs and the CIRA camera crew set up next to the TV cameras. They searched all over for the Restless Arm Syndrome banner. They started filming, Laguna's actions unnoticed in the background.

The boom truck moved down the line, and four more protesters easily gave up and climbed into the bucket. Laguna groped the girls and elbowed the boys.

LeBron, now the only one left in a tree, went on shouting defiantly. The TV cameras saw a large African-American man, unafraid and challenging the police. "Whose town is this?" he shouted. "Stop them! Save the trees. Join us. Stop the rape of the earth!"

Laguna rode the bucket up to LeBron. LeBron swung away on his climbing rope. Laguna took out his pepper spray can and sprayed a good blast at LeBron. LeBron ducked behind the Greenwerks banner.

"Cut that sign down," Croakie ordered over the radio.

Laguna heard. He reached out and grabbed for the banner. LeBron snatched the banner away. Laguna grabbed again. This time he held on, and the two of them had a tug of war. LeBron hung from his rope harness, one hand holding the banner, the other clutched on the bullhorn.

Laguna maneuvered the bucket closer. He grabbed at LeBron's bullhorn hand. LeBron yanked it away and the bullhorn flew through the air towards the crowd. It clunked a policeman on the back of his riot helmet. The policeman's head went forward an inch or two and he recovered immediately. They exchanged words. They both looked up at LeBron.

Croakie saw it all. He saw the bullhorn fly through the air. He saw it hit the policeman. He called the Chief of Police.

"Get that officer to the emergency room."

"I think he's OK, Mayor. It hit him in the helmet."

"Assault on an officer – use your head, numbskull. I want that kid in the tree charged with assault. Call the District Attorney. I want that officer taken to the emergency room."

The Chief didn't answer for a long moment.

"Whatever you say, Mayor."

Croakie picked up his cell phone. "Bonnie. Get a TV crew from each station down to the Emergency Room. An officer is coming down. I want it covered. Call the District Attorney. I want this protester charged Monday morning." He hung up.

Laguna now had LeBron, still hanging from his harness, handcuffed. Before loading LeBron in the bucket, Laguna blasted him with pepper spray. LeBron screamed.

Fawn Fallingsnow had a perfect view, and caught every detail.

Grey Pearce, towing his Girl Scouts, finally elbowed and fought his way in front of the TV cameras. He lined them up. Success! The Restless Arm Syndrome banner – held by Girl Scouts, no less – was in front of three local TV cameras.

A voice shouted from a police bullhorn: "Clear the area. All people clear the block. Clear the block now. Disperse or be arrested."

The girls dropped their banner and walked off. "Noooo!" Grey wailed after them.

The TV crews, following orders, backed down the street.

The protest was over. Most people cleared out. A few hung back to shout at the police and a couple more were arrested, but the energy was gone. Only the police, Mayor Croakie and a few bystanders were left.

Fawn Fallingsnow quietly left with her camera.

Grey found Bugs a block away. "How much did we get of the banner, Bugs?"

"Ten, fifteen seconds, max."

"Shit. Let's get back to the Institute. I've got to call the stations. Those fifteen seconds could put us two months ahead on our marketing campaign for Restless Arm. We'll get a big bonus if we can create this disease in record time."

Laguna walked over to Croakie's Cadillac. He pulled open the passenger door. He was sweating and still breathing hard. He started to sit down.

"Hey, don't put your feet on the floor," said Croakie. "Keep your feet outside the car."

Laguna leaned over and looked in. He didn't get in the car. "What the fuck you mean? The floor's covered in peanut shells."

"Them I can sweep out. Your feet are greasy."

"They're clean."

Croakie looked around to see who might be watching. "I don't want to be seen with you, Victor. Go away."

"What the fuck. I been seen with you before. I been seen with Beatrice, every inch of her. Her and me. You loved it."

"That's different. Go away."

Laguna, furious, slammed the door and walked off.

Croakie got out of his Caddy. He looked around. I need a kid with me for this interview, he thought. Gotta have a kid for this interview. He saw a young couple with a baby in a stroller. Perfect.

Croakie went up to them. They recognized him, of course. Croakie bent over to the child. "What's your name, honey?

"Alexy."

He looked at the parents. "Can I hold her?" At their nod, Croakie picked up the child. His skin crawled at the touch, as it always did. "Big Art loves kids" was his election slogan. Any time he could, he appeared on camera with a child. He read to kids at kindergarten in front of TV cameras. He spoke at schools. He held kids in his lap.

He hated every second of it. He hated the smell of kids. He hated their sticky little fingers. He hated their voices. He hated their doting parents.

As he approached the TV cameras, he kept a "Big Art Croakie loves kids" smile on his face. The child started messing with his face. No! Not the face! he screamed to himself. Please not the hair, he silently pleaded to the child, please not the hair.

The kid went for the hair. Croakie kept a "Big Art Croakie Loves Kids" smile on his face.

"Ready when you are, Mayor," said a reporter.

Croakie hugged the child in tight. "These protesters, these ecoterrorists are a menace. Today they sent a decorated officer to the hospital." He looked at the child and made a gitchy-goo smile.

"This protest cost the City thousands of dollars in police overtime pay. That money has to come from somewhere. Where does it come from? It comes from programs to help kids like little Alexy here." The cameras zoomed in for a final shot.

Croakie handed the child quickly back to her parents and hustled back to his Caddy. He took out a bottle of antibacterial gel and rubbed it on his hands. He rubbed it on his face and into his hair. He shuddered.

Back at The Columbia Institute for Research Analysis, Grey Pearce called one of the TV station managers.

"Bill, this is Grey. I need a favor."

Grey took in a breath. He leaned back in his chair and released it.

"We buy a lot of ad time for NanoPharm pharmaceuticals from you. Well, I need your help now."

"What can I do?"

"At the end of your filming of the tree-sitters' protest downtown, we put a NanoPharm banner announcing a new drug in front of the camera. It's a great shot. Two Girl Scouts holding it up. Beautiful. About 15 seconds. Could you put that shot on tonight's evening news?"

"Uh... sorry, Grey. We already have our story."

"You do?"

"We're going with the Mayor and the police on this."

Grey shook his head in disbelief. "What's that?"

"Our lead is 'Protesters attack police.' We have footage of this black kid in a tree throwing a bullhorn and striking an officer... in the head, no less. The officer went to the hospital. We're covering the hospital too. That's our story. We aren't running anything else."

He called the other two stations – same result. They were going with the Mayor and police.

Grey hung up. He was deflated. They were going to have to convince the public it had Restless Arm Syndrome – a condition that had never existed before in history– the old-fashioned way, one massive ad buy at a time.

Back at the Greenwerks office, Fawn Fallingsnow downloaded all her video footage to her laptop and sent copies to a dozen trusted friends. She scanned the tape on fast-forward until she found the shot of Laguna grabbing Tara by the crotch, and the shot of Laguna spraying pepper spray in the face of a handcuffed LeBron Booker. She called the thirty-second film "Police Brutality in Eugene" and put it up on YouTube. She also made a ten-minute tape of the protest that included all the arrests, and put it all on Facebook. Before closing her laptop, she sent links to several thousand environmental sympathizers throughout the Pacific Northwest.

CHAPTER 8

"She said she wasn't feeling so good. So I went over to set up the lawn sprinkler for her."

"Is she OK?"

Doyle glanced over at Malcolm. Malcolm's head was down and his hand was on his cheek, patting gently. "You can ask her about it. I'm worried."

"She'll be all right, Malcolm. You'll see. She'll make us tea, same as usual, and we'll talk about the garden and the birds."

They crossed the street and knocked on the door of a well-kept little cottage with roses blooming in the front yard. In a moment Ms. Cup stood before them, beaming warmth and love.

At five foot three inches, with curly graying hair, Ms. Sara Cup was a force of nature. Her strength and caring had saved Malcolm and many other sensitive souls from being beaten down by a hostile school environment.

A friend of Malcolm's mother, it was Ms. Cup who suggested Malcolm come join her at the private school where she taught. And there it was that Malcolm flourished under her nourishing and protective vigilance. Malcolm was closer to her than he was to anyone else, including his mom.

"Doyle! It's so good to see you. It's been a while." She shuffled over to the kitchen counter, filled the kettle and put it on. "You must tell me what you have been doing since I saw you last."

"I've just been working at the Nexus Lounge, same as usual." Doyle watched Ms. Cup trying not to show her difficulty in taking down the teapot and mugs. He glanced at Malcolm to see if he'd noticed it too, and saw a deep sadness on his face.

Still, she smiled. "I grew the most wonderful verbena last year. Absolutely a bumper crop. Smell this." She stuck the large jar in their faces. "Strong, isn't it? I'm going to make a whole pot and we'll have some cookies. Doyle, would you mind putting these placemats on the table and moving that big cookie jar there where we can reach it?"

They sat and she poured the tea. "Please grab some cookies, boys; I can't possibly eat them all myself. There's lemon and a few oatmeal."

Doyle hesitated, but then spoke up. "Ms. Cup, it seems like you're moving a little slow these days."

She looked, not at Doyle, but at Malcolm – the one she knew would have the hardest time watching her decline. "It's not so bad, really. Just some aches and pains. Hard to reach, hard to bend, oh, and maybe I'm a bit more forgetful lately. So don't worry about me, I've been growing some herbs in the garden that I've read about that can help me with it." She reached out to Malcolm and covered his hand with hers. "It's a natural thing, Malcolm. Just part of getting old. Happens to us all, someday."

She turned to Doyle and smiled. "Let's talk about something pleasanter. Do you see much of your old school friends, Doyle? Do you know what they're up to?"

"Almost everyone's moved away. I mostly work, but I still like to play the guitar and write the occasional song."

"Is there a young lady in your life?"

"I wish! I guess I just haven't met the right one. I was dating a while back but we broke up. Who knows, maybe I'll meet somebody tonight."

Ms. Cup poured more tea into all the cups. Steam rose.

"You know," said Doyle, "if you ever need any help around here, you can just call my new cell number. Or if there's an emergency. I only live up on the hill; I can be here in a couple of minutes."

"That's very sweet of you, and I just may call on you for help when I clean out the garage." She passed a pad and pen to him and looked at Malcolm. "I already have your number, Malcolm. You always help me."

Malcolm smiled for the first time since they had arrived. She leaned over and patted him on his back, knowing how he loved to be touched by the few people he trusted. He took the opportunity of her nearness to smell her deeply, intuiting her metabolic situation on a visceral level. He followed the unique fragrance like a bloodhound into a web of sequential reactions. He momentarily disappeared from the present, to follow his nano-vision to the healing place.

Noticing that Malcolm had drifted away and guessing the reason, Doyle maintained the chitchat with Ms. Cup, but she relieved him of that duty shortly. "Well, boys, it has been a wonderful visit and I hope you come again very soon, but I just ran myself a hot bath and was ready to step into it when you arrived. The hot bath really helps me these days."

The boys stood to go. "Put pine needles in the tub. It will help you," said Malcolm.

"You know, it's interesting you suggest that, Malcolm. The druggist gave me a bottle of fir needle oil for the bath last week. It really feels good."

Ms. Cup smiled at him like a summer dawn, and he smiled back. They hugged her goodbye and walked across the street. Malcolm was calm.

"See, she's just fine," Doyle said.

"I can help her," Malcolm nodded. "I know I can help her."

CHAPTER 9

The phone rang for the fifth time, echoing off the empty walls of the rental house on Grant near 10th. It was a big house, with plenty of room for Fawn and her young son Clive. He had already fallen asleep in her arms. She put him down.

"Hello, this is Fawn."

"I, well, I got your name in the bar yesterday and…"

"Oh, you're Benny. Hey, good to meet you last night, we have some exciting things planned and the next meeting is on Thursday so you…"

"Ah, no, wait, wait, it's not Benny. Ah… my name is Doyle, I work with Benny, I tend bar, I saw you at the Nexus last night. I, uh, you've never been in the Nexus before have you? I'm sorry I just kept staring at you last night…"

"Oh, hi. Well, I did see you last night. I would have come over to the bar but I was with the group and we were doing a lot of planning and I just couldn't get over to chat. But I did see you looking at me."

"Sorry, I was staring, wasn't I? I know it's rude. I guess I wanted to meet you and couldn't get out from behind the bar. I'm usually not rude."

"Well, come to the meeting on Thursday, if you like, and we can talk then."

"I thought maybe we could meet for a cup of coffee or some lunch or something, I mean if you feel like it. I mean, I know you don't know me. I don't know, I thought maybe you'd be up for a cup of coffee or something."

Fawn chuckled at his nervousness. "It's OK, Doyle. I think it would be nice to meet for coffee. I'm free today all day. I have to wait for my son to be ready for his nap, so, I can meet you around two?"

"That would be perfect; we could meet at The Laughing Planet on Blair, if that's good for you. You need a ride?"

"No, that's near my house. I'll walk there with the stroller. I'll see you at two."

"Great, see you then."

Doyle felt oddly at ease. His hands weren't sweaty. He was elated, looking forward to the meeting.

Fawn hung up the phone and spun, her hair and sundress whirling out around her. "Yessss!"

Laughing Planet was crowded for lunch. Fawn noticed that all the tables were filled. Patrons from all walks of Eugene life lined up to place their orders at the register. Doyle waved from a table, and Fawn pushed the stroller over.

She began talking as soon as she sat down. "My son's name is Clive. It's a proper British name, after his dad's dad. That's where Roy was from. We met in college, University of Washington. We were both in journalism school. Royston Elwood. He'd always wanted to come to the states. I was on scholarship from the Iroquois Nation. On my father's side, I qualified for the money. My last name is Fallingsnow."

She glanced away to Clive in his stroller napping. "He loves his nap. He's a great napper." She shook her head and picked at her cinnamon roll.

Dutch sipped his cappuccino. "So what happened, if I can ask?"

She took a deep breath. "He was killed." She shook her head. "He never got to see his son. That was almost three years ago now. I was running the camera and he was interviewing a policeman. Everything was going OK, and then the crowd of protesters surged and he was pushed down. I fell too, but he didn't make it. His skull was broken. I still have the footage, it was like a wave of people, and when it subsided a few of us were on the ground. Roy never got up."

"I'm so sorry, Fawn." Doyle reached out and touched her forearm.

She looked out the window, drifting, then brought her eyes back to his. "It just made me harder and stronger, more dedicated. I don't want to ever think that he wasted his life, that the cause of human rights is not valuable."

She sipped her tea and smiled. She talked about her life as a single mother, helping at Greenwerks and trying to make a meager living as a commissioned sales rep for a German company with strong environmental principles called VertBild.

"Really? I never heard of them," said Doyle.

"VertBild invests in green remodeling. Eventually green remodeling becomes green rentals and green home sales that will continue supporting VertBild investors in perpetuity. That's the plan, anyway." Her smile was without cynicism.

"Sounds like a great idea."

"It is, and I get a place to live for free in whatever remodel they are working on. What about you? What are you up to? I've been doing all the talking here. You haven't said a thing. And which do you go by, Doyle or Dutch?"

"Whichever you like is fine. I've lived here all my life...." He continued his story with details about his school, his friends, guitar-playing, songwriting and drawing, about getting a little too involved in drugs, then getting out, up to the more recent events in his life.

Clive napped hard through the lunch hour. They talked and sipped and snacked until Doyle realized he needed to get ready for his shift. "I hate to run, but I really must."

Fawn stood and gave him a hug. It was sweet and warm.

"I'm glad I met you, Dutch. I'd like to make dinner for you tomorrow. Would you like that?"

"I would indeed." The hug held just a moment longer than social politeness dictated, and Clive stirred.

The hours passed like days for Doyle as he anticipated his dinner with Fawn. Finally the time came, and he stood in her kitchen sipping a local beer and watched her move gracefully about the stove.

"Once Roy was gone my mind was made up. I became committed even more to activism and resistance. I did it for me, for Roy's memory, for everyone who gets the shaft from predatory capitalism."

Doyle set the table. Clive watched him from the playpen. The house was in partial disarray. On the shady side of the house, light tubes were put into the ceiling. On the sunny side, a solar array was being installed. Ladders and brackets and wood stood alongside the house. The backyard had been excavated to accommodate some kind of buried pipes that would take advantage of the earth's constant temperature. It was mostly over Doyle's head.

"This house is going to be a showcase for VertBild's remodel program. We're only a few months away."

"It's a great idea."

He opened the wine and poured while Fawn brought out dinner. Clive contentedly played, cooed and occasionally shrieked.

Fawn continued explaining and Doyle happily watched her animated eyes and her lovely lips while she talked. He was captivated and delighted. He would have been happy if she'd recited names from the phone book.

It was getting to be time to leave.

"I really like you. I am profoundly attracted to you. I just can't take my eyes away from you. I could sit and watch you all day and night," confessed Doyle, like a lovelorn teen.

She stepped forward into his arms and they kissed.

CHAPTER 10

"Silence!" Judge Carl Hibben banged his gavel. He glared over his reading glasses at the unruly crowd of Greenwerks spectators in his courtroom. He banged again.

"Order!" he shouted into his microphone. Bang.

The grumbling stopped.

"One more outburst and I will empty this courtroom. Am I clear?" His fierce look challenged the room. Nobody spoke. He nodded to the court reporter.

"The Court will hear final arguments in the matter of reducing bail for LeBron Booker, charged with Assault with a Dangerous Weapon, Obstruction of Justice, Resisting Arrest and Disorderly Conduct. Defense attorney, do you have anything to say?"

The young court-appointed defense attorney shook his head, no. LeBron Booker, dressed in a faded green jumpsuit and wearing handcuffs, elbowed his lawyer hard.

LeBron looked both angry and terrified. Mayor Croakie smiled from his front row seat.

"C'mon, be a fuckin' lawyer, do something!" shouted someone from the crowd.

Bang! "Order!"

The defense attorney sighed, avoiding his client's glare. He picked up his notes and stood. His frown said plainly, three years of law school and $90,000 in student loans for the privilege of earning a flat fee of $150 for this crummy hearing.

"Your Honor," he said, "the state bail guidelines recommend no more than $100,000. The District Attorney has somehow convinced the bail custodians to call for $250,000, which is arbitrary and capricious."

48

He sat down, and folded his arms across his chest. LeBron's mouth dropped. That's all?

Judge Hibben frowned at the feeble argument. John Tulley, the thrice-elected District Attorney, turned around in his chair and winked at Mayor Croakie.

Grumble, grumble. Bang! "Order!"

"Very well. The court rules that bail for LeBron Booker is set at $250,000. Mr. Booker can only be released from custody if he provides 10% of the bail money."

LeBron elbowed his lawyer.

The lawyer half stood. "I object." He sat down.

"Take it to the Court of Appeals, Counselor. I look forward to reading your brief." The judge leaned back in his chair. "Till then, the ruling stands." He banged his gavel. "Court adjourned."

The courtroom erupted with boos and catcalls. "Bailiff, clear the court!"

Three burly deputies advanced from behind the judge. The Greenwerks protesters turned for the door.

The Judge left. So did the defense attorney. He didn't look at his client.

LeBron's handcuffs and leg cuffs were secured to a belt manacle. A guard frog-marched him out a side door.

The Mayor and his aide stayed in the Courtroom. Croakie waved at an assistant district attorney leaving the room.

"How are your kids doing?" Croakie called.

"Croakie loves kids!" The ADA gave the Mayor a thumbs-up salute.

"Croakie loves kids!" Big Art bellowed out to the room, a winner's smile on his broad, powerful face.

As soon as everyone was gone, the smile melted away. He took out a comb and prepared for the TV cameras outside the courtroom door.

"Excuse me for a second, Mayor," said his aide. "I'm gonna get the kids for today's TV shot. I'll be right back." Croakie straightened his tie.

The aide returned with two young parents carrying towheaded blond twins wearing white dresses. Croakie froze. He greeted the parents and made smiley faces at the girls.

"Oh, I just can't believe it. My babies are going to be on TV!" said the woman in a rising, high-pitched voice. All Croakie heard was: eeeeeeeeek.

"Could, uh, you wait outside, please?" he asked the parents.

"I'm so excited...my babieeees..."

Eeeeeeeeek.

Croakie smiled a "Big Art Croakie loves kids" smile and waved goodbye. The moment they were gone, he grabbed the young aide by the lapels and pushed him against the wall. "You dumbfuck, worthless, shit-for-brains dickhead."

The aide's head bobbled back and forth.

"Wha, wha... what's the problem?"

"Problem? You don't see the fucking problem?"

"W-what?"

"The kids, goddammit! You don't see the problem with those fucking kids?"

"They... they look adorable."

"Yeah, they're adorable, totally adorable, and..." Croakie lowered his voice for effect – "They're white. They're blonde. They're dressed in white dresses. And you want me to be on TV with those white girls while I get tough on crime, using a black kid as public enemy number one? They'll call me a racist, you dumb jerkoff."

Croakie released the quaking young man in disgust. "I can't fuckin' believe this. Big Art Croakie fucking loves godammed kids, and you're going to fuck up my camera shot right in an election year. This will be my first time with no kids in a TV shot, and it's all your fault. Idiot."

The aide started to leave, but Croakie's beefy hand fell hard on his shoulder and he reluctantly turned back. "Get me a black kid. Yeah. Any black people in the office have kids? Come on, think!"

"Uh, let's see," said the aide. "Oh yeah, there's Letisha, she has kids. Uh – oh, wait – she's on vacation. Sorry."

"Brown. I'll take brown. Any brown kids? How about Hispanic? Asian? Anybody."

A TV crewman tapped on the window of the courtroom for Mayor Croakie – 30 seconds till airtime.

"You fucked me on this. I'll get you," Croakie snarled.

"Wait. Mayor, there's something else you should know."

"What now?" Croakie turned back.

The aide, who figured this job was lost anyway, delivered the bad news. "A student TV station in Chapel Hill North Carolina broadcast a second tape of the protest. It doesn't support our version of events at all."

"What do I care about a college TV station in North Carolina? That's nothing. Get a fuckin' brain, wussy."

Croakie put on his smile and stepped through the courtroom door towards the lights. The parents with the kids pounced from both sides. They put a blond kid in each arm in full view of the TV cameras. Trapped!

He smiled. He felt the girls' busy, hot hands on him. Oh my God. Don't touch my hair. Anything but the hair! Mayor Croakie smiled and moved to the microphone. All he could feel was twenty sticky little fingers in his hair.

His chuckle felt forced even to him. All that came to him was his prepared speech.

"LeBron Booker is a violent criminal. He is a menace, an eco-terrorist, and a danger to all the good folks of Eugene. I promise you: as long as I'm Mayor, I will keep the streets safe from unwelcome criminals like him. You got my word on it. I'll fight to make our little city safe for little Kaitlin and Kayla here, because – Croakie loves kids." He paused and hugged the children, who had tired of his hair and were pulling his tie.

A reporter pushed to the front. "Any comment on the second video of the event? Have you seen it?"

"No. I haven't seen it. But I'm sure it supports our position that LeBron Booker is a common criminal and a menace. Good riddance." Croakie knew it was time to go. "That's all for today. Remember: Croakie loves kids!" He set the kids down, and left quickly towards the restroom.

CHAPTER 11

In the bathroom, Croakie pulled off his coat and hung it over a stall. He threw his tie in the garbage, and took off his shirt. He splashed hot water over his face and head. He shuddered. Why do they always have to touch my hair?

The aide came in. He locked the door and took a towel out of his briefcase. Croakie held his hand out, and the aide gave him the towel.

"Where did this second tape come from?"

"It looks like a woman named Fawn Fallingsnow took the video. I Googled her and she's one of the Greenwerks protesters. Her name is on lots of videos for Greenwerks, including this one. Mayor, I've seen it. It's not good."

"I was there. What do you mean?"

"It doesn't show LeBron Booker throwing a bullhorn. The bullhorn kind of flew out of his hand when Laguna was wrestling with him in the tree and pepper spraying him. It was an accident. And the cop? He didn't even register that he'd been hit, until another officer told him."

Croakie pulled his attention away from himself in the mirror, turned and glared. "Call Detective Laguna," he snapped. "Tell him to meet me at the Nexus tonight. Tell him I've got a job for him."

The aide was silent. He chewed his lower lip. "Uh, are you sure, Mayor?"

Croakie immediately stopped drying his face. When the towel came away, his eyes were furious slits. His lips were stretched into a mean, tight line.

His voice was acid, ice cold. "Are you questioning me?"

"I, I guess not."

Croakie threw the towel at him.

"She's gotta take that video off the Internet. Tell Laguna, whatever it takes." He pointed at the door.

"Get outta here."

CHAPTER 12

An oversized housefly buzzed in giant slow circles around Greenwerks' headquarters and finally landed on a computer screen. It wobbled a little as it crawled, a huge body on spindly legs, like a donkey carrying a load of bricks.

Fawn Fallingsnow was watching her computer screen, waiting for the TV news. She picked up a magazine. She cursed the jerk who didn't close the door and she batted the fly hard. The big fly sailed off and landed in a corner. It twitched its tiny legs in the air, and lay still. After a while, it twitched some more, then turned over, righted itself, and took off into the air.

"How the fuck are we gonna come up with $25,000 fucking dollars?" said a heavyset boy covered with piercings and dressed in black.. He was sitting on the floor next to the wall, leaning on his backpack.

"I don't know," said Macrouder, sprawled on a couch behind Fawn. He was watching her computer screen for the TV news too. "We only have $1500."

"Shit. We need more than $25,000," said a woman dressed in tan shorts and expensive hiking boots. "We need to hire a real attorney for LeBron, not that useless public defender."

"I have no idea where we can get that kind of money," said Macrouder glumly. "LeBron is truly fucked."

"How about a benefit concert?" said the skinny girl. "My sister's boyfriend is the lead singer of the Cosmic Bees."

Macrouder sat up. "Now that's a good idea. That's a real decent idea." He stood. "But aren't the Cosmic Bees on tour?"

"Nope. I saw the lead singer yesterday. I'll talk to my sister about it."

"Good. Concert it is. I'll secure the permit," said Macrouder.

The room came alive with everyone talking at once about planning the benefit concert when Fawn said, "Shhhhhhhh. The news is on. Maybe they'll finally show our protest video."

"Fat fuckin' chance of that," said the heavy boy.

"I heard that Fawn's video aired in Boulder last night," said another kid.

"Shhhhhhhh, here it is."

A reporter stood on the courtroom steps. "Here, in today's top story, Mayor Croakie stands up for law and order, and against criminal behavior, at the courthouse..."

The TV showed Croakie holding two adorable kids, who were busy giving him a new hairdo.

"...LeBron Booker is a violent criminal. He is a menace, an eco-terrorist, and a danger to all the good folks of Eugene. I promise you. As long as I'm Mayor, I will keep the streets safe from unwelcome criminals like him. You got my word on it. I'll fight to make our little city safe for little Kaitlin and Kayla here, because – Croakie loves kids."

The TV news switched to another story, a traffic accident on the interstate. Fawn muted the sound.

Macrouder sat down. "That's all they're gonna show. They're twisting the story and making LeBron the sacrificial fall guy. It's political theater, fully staged to unite the community for Three Minutes of Hate, all directed at LeBron, the symbolic criminal menace of the day. Let's everybody shout 'good riddance', celebrate for thirty seconds, then on to that next new celebrity scandal." Somebody's dog wandered around the room, stalking the large buzzy fly.

"Democracy has become absurd political theater, a lifeless farce," said Macrouder. "The real facts don't matter, only the manufactured image." He opened a bottle of carrot juice and swigged. "Debate is replaced with distraction. Politics is just another manipulated product. Democracy is a joke. The consumers are fed a false sense of psychological superiority over the latest bogeyman, in this case LeBron, who fits their stereotype: a dangerous young black man. For a short time the public gets to feel good about themselves at the expense of the

56

bogeyman. Meanwhile, the corporate state is picking their pockets clean."

Fawn, who had heard it all before, wasn't listening. She had brought up the video clip of Croakie's news conference. She also brought up LeBron Booker's police mug shot, showing him as a very sad and frightened young man with a swollen cheek and a red eye. She pasted the mug shot into the upper left corner of the Croakie news conference, so that the mug shot was next to Croakie and the two girls throughout his speech. Perfect. Choke on that, Croakie. She up-linked the doctored clip of the news conference to everyone on the Greenwerks email list. While she was at it, she up-linked it to Facebook and to YouTube, and she sent a copy to Black Educational TV. When she was done, she sat back and pondered who else to send it to.

An idea came to her. It was a long shot, but what the hell. She Googled the email address for Reverend Ron Hawkins, civil rights activist and onetime presidential candidate from Harlem, New York.

She emailed Reverend Hawkins her video of Croakie's news conference. She also sent him the video of LeBron struggling with Laguna in the tree during the protest.

As she packed up her laptop, she called over to Macrouder: "Don't forget – dinner at my place tomorrow. I want you guys to meet my friend Doyle."

CHAPTER 13

"Reverend, there's something here I think you should see." A well-dressed, middle-aged black woman stood in the door of Reverend Ron Hawkins' office in a handsome brownstone on West 129th and 7th Avenue in Harlem. Behind her stood four other employees.

Hawkins looked up. His broad fleshy face, slicked back curly hair, heavy eyebrows and thin mustache were framed by the picture window behind him.

"What is it?" Hawkins put down his busy travel itinerary: protests regarding unionized workers, a press conference on Capitol Hill, appearances on various regional and national talk shows, both radio and TV.

Hawkins didn't preach to a church congregation anymore. Except for special occasions in his old storefront church, his days behind the pulpit were over. He devoted his time to his causes, the most prominent of which was drawing attention to himself. His hot-blooded, indignant face was instantly recognizable throughout America.

On a shelf next to him, an old Golden Gloves boxing trophy sat in front of a boxing poster showing a young Hawkins with slicked back hair: Kid Hawkins, flyweight division. That was many years and many fatty casseroles and rich desserts ago.

Hawkins was tough and he was undaunted by criticism. He had once run for Mayor of New York and lost. In the next election he ran for Governor as a third party candidate and lost worse. After that he ran for President as a Democrat and appeared in several debates. He won less than 1% of caucus votes in Iowa and dropped out.

Ron Hawkins considered all of this part of his greater plan for success. The walls of his office were covered with photos of himself with every important person willing to stand and be photographed with him, including the Pope, Democratic presidents, politicians, world leaders, Mother Theresa, movie stars and black glitterati.

"Reverend, I just forwarded an email to your computer from a woman named Fawn Fallingsnow, in Eugene, Oregon. I think you might want to see this."

His employees moved into the room. They had all seen the video.

Hawkins frowned and turned to his computer. He found the link to the video clip. He leaned back in the huge chair that dwarfed his heavy 5'6" frame. He played the clip of Croakie's news conference and frowned deeply. He leaned forward, fully attentive, and watched the protest footage. He saw LeBron struggling in the tree. He saw the bullhorn fly out of his hands during the struggle and saw it bounce off a police officer's helmet.

Hawkins replayed both tapes again. His fingers were drumming on the desk top. He shook his head back and forth. "Mmmmm, this is some serious shit."

"I hear ya, Reverend," said an aide, nodding her head. "Serious shit."

"Who's this motherfuckin' Croakie think he is?" Hawkins' lower lip stuck out pugnaciously.

"Yeah, Reverend."

"Word."

Hawkins lapsed into preacher-speak. His voice rose to its full volume. "This some seeeerious shit. Jim Croakie bringing back the KKK. Sending this black kid to prison over some... bullshit... some... nasty... bullshit. This is a modern-day lynching. We know what this Croakie's trying to do – he's sending a message to black folks – get outta our white supremacist paradise in Eugene, Oregon."

"I hear you. Mm hmm." The aides were nodding and murmuring like a congregation.

"Cancel the Indiana appearance," said Hawkins. "This some serious shit in the heartland of the Aryan Nation. Get me on a plane to Oregon tomorrow morning. Get me information on this Croakie motherfucker. I wanna know all about this Aryan cracker."

Hawkins paused. "And find out who my man LeBron's people are. Get me their phone numbers."

The aides took notes.

"I'm gonna open up a big black can of whoop-ass on Jim KKK Croakie. I'm gonna bring some shit back on them white supremacists... trying to tell black folks they can't live in the Pacific Northwest. I'm putting my black foot up the ass of the Aryan Nation."

"Are you flying out alone on this?" asked an aide.

"Hell no, this is too important," Hawkins snapped back. "Full entourage. We are all going, my friends. We shall all be there for God's greater glory."

CHAPTER 14

Doyle sipped the last of his cooling cappuccino. He began to hum again. His song remained incomplete.

He knelt before the secondary bottle collection behind the bar. The vanilla vodka was depleted, nothing else.

"How's it going Dutch?" Doyle's startled head jerked up and almost hit the shelf.

"Shit. Don't creep up on me like that, Benny. You scared the shit out of me. But then I'm sure you already know that, don't you. It's what you wanted. I know, very funny..." Doyle went back to his bottles.

"Ah come on, Dutchie, it's just a joke. Give you a little jump," said Benny apologetically.

"How was your date?" said Benny, tying his apron.

"How'd you know about that?"

"I know everything, but don't tell me yet. I'm gonna get my sandwich and you can tell me while I eat."

"Sure, man. I'll be happy to be your personal entertainment. You can even watch me wipe down my counter."

Moments after Benny left for the kitchen, the dreaded Kenny Gee came on quietly in the background. In twenty minutes the first happy hour wave would come in. Benny slid onto a seat at the counter and worked on a BLT while Dutch confessed his love for Fawn.

"She's a real beauty, Dutch. Don't get your heart broken," he warned.

The conversation lasted as long as the sandwich. Doyle's story was convenient for Benny, like daytime TV.

"Well, I'll go wash my plate."

"While you're at it, get rid of Kenny Gee."

"Why? He's the world's best jazz sax player. He's a master."

"Just change it, Benny, or you'll never see that CD again."

Seconds after Benny left for the kitchen, Victor Laguna walked in. He looked from side to side, as if the bar were full and he had to guard a private conversation.

He grabbed his own lapels and adjusted them by lifting and lowering them several times.

He leaned in close to Doyle.

He jutted his chin.

He cocked his head.

Dutch knew what was coming next – the squeeze. How often had he seen this?

Victor Laguna was like a chicken looking one-eyed at the earth for the emergence of a worm; there was a cold menace in his dead eyes. "Whattya got for me?"

"Oh hey, Vic, how about a cup of coffee or a drink? Maybe something from the kitchen?"

"Sure, pal, I'll just sit down and you can fix me something to go."

Dutch turned and called in the order.

"So, how about it? You've been putting me off for two weeks now. That last chicken-shit bust won't get you very far, you know. Teenagers with a few joints are not of interest to my superior officers, Doyle. But a bartender with a full page of blotter LSD is still a good bust. I've held up my side of the deal, but you, you've been taking your fuckin' time, Dutchie."

"Look, Vic, I always come through for you, don't I? I always get you something. It's just been a little dry lately, that's all. Look at this place. You're the only one here!"

"You better make it happen, or I'll put you into the system today. You hear me?" Laguna stuck his forefinger into Doyle's chest and poked a few times.

Benny set the bag of food onto the counter, took one look, turned and left.

"I'll be back before you know it, and you better have something or we're taking a walk." Laguna stood up, his chin jutting, well within Doyle's body space..

"OK, OK," said Doyle.

Laguna turned and left. Like a ghost, Benny appeared where Laguna had just been standing.

"I've seen Laguna's act before, Doyle. What's the deal?"

Doyle's heart was pounding with fear and anger. He shook his head and slapped the bar with his moist bar towel. "Fuckin' guy. Still a bully, now he's a cop."

"What's he got on you?"

"It was ten months ago, a real busy Saturday night. You weren't here that night. Some chick was kind of coming on to me. She handed me a piece of paper. I thought it was her phone number and stuck it in my pocket. She left. Fifteen minutes later, Laguna hauls me outside to the parking lot, puts the cuffs on me and finds a full page of blotter acid. A fuckin' setup. Now he's squeezing me for info on the drug scene or else he'll take me in and process the arrest. I got no choice. I'm fucked. His word against mine."

"What a bastard. He's been that way since we were kids. Sorry."

"I keep giving him minor stuff, but he wants something big. I don't know anyone big. I'm just a bartender. He thinks I'm his ticket to a promotion." Doyle shook his head. "I don't want to go to jail, Benny."

They were interrupted by a group of six women walking in and sitting at their favorite table. "Five old fashioneds and a white wine spritzer for the book club," Benny murmured to Doyle before he turned to greet the group.

Benny turned chirped, "The usual for you lovely ladies?"

"Hi, Benny, yes, give us the usual," they chorused.

Benny turned to Doyle, caught his eye and nodded. Doyle had already started making the drinks.

CHAPTER 15

Malcolm pushed back his chair and looked up at the enormous TV screen on the wall above his desk at The Institute. He locked eyes with the eyes of a moray eel peeking out of a coral reef.

He wanted a better look at its teeth. He pushed back his chair and put on his 3D glasses and ear buds. In an instant he was floating. Waves broke gently on the tropical reef. He saw wickedly sharp teeth, and a mouth that could swallow a fist. The breaking waves filled the blue water and the entire room with shimmering light.

This TV in the storeroom at the Columbia Institute of Research Analysis played an endless loop of tropical reef world. Malcolm knew that he did his best thinking floating like this, in the blueness of a coral reef.

It was Sunday morning, his favorite day at work. Sunday he had The Institute all to himself.

Today was also a special Sunday. Today he was testing two new pharmaceuticals for NanoPharm. He loved this creative testing and exploring. He wished that NanoPharm could bring him new challenges every day, and grieved that they only created a handful of new drugs each year for him to test.

Malcolm was the only known nano-savant in the world. CIRA had been created around him. CIRA was located on Friendly Street in Eugene, because Malcolm lived on Friendly Street and Malcolm didn't like to travel.

Malcolm had an encyclopedic memory of every molecule he had ever smelled since he was a child. It was all in there, whether he looked at it or not. He started analyzing molecules and elements early in life. He read chemistry and physics books when he was five. He mastered Internet research at eight.

When he was ten, Malcolm's parents enrolled their strange child in the Eugene Arts and Science Academy, a private school endowed by NanoPharm's founder, Bill Dhey. Malcolm flourished there, but his parents worried about him and had their lawyer draw up a severe, penalty-laden non-disclosure agreement. Every teacher at the school was required to sign it. Every NanoPharm employee who knew of Malcolm signed it. Bill Dhey, the sole shareholder of NanoPharm, signed it.

They had all agreed to basically the same thing: to shut the fuck up. No newspaper stories, no interviews, no videotaping, no recording, no emails with his name, no talking to family members including spouse, no typing his name into any computer. So by the time Malcolm graduated from Eugene Arts and Sciences Academy he knew more science than a roomful of PhDs. He never set foot in a classroom again.

Now 32, he still enjoyed a relatively private life.

But today, on one of his special Sundays, a day of exploration into two new pharmaceuticals, Malcolm couldn't find joy in this tropical reef. He couldn't concentrate on the bookkeeping, a chore he performed for CIRA so he wouldn't have to share his stockroom office with a bookkeeper.

Malcolm was worried about Ms. Cup. She was sick. He wanted to help her, and he didn't know how.

Malcolm decided to postpone the bookkeeping and get straight to the good stuff: analyzing the two new pharmaceuticals, Torpidan and Epithet.

He took off his 3D glasses. He pulled the two boxes of pills off the shelf.

Something was wrong. Something was off. He opened the boxes and pulled out the paperwork. The first document read ".5 Kilo, Torpidan." Impossible, thought Malcolm. The box is too large. The documents for the second box read ".5 kilo, Epithet." He hefted the box. Too heavy.

Malcolm emptied the boxes. Each held 10 large bottles of pills. Each bottle weighed .5 kilos. Oops, thought Malcolm. NanoPharm had over-shipped the Torpidan and Epithet. They'd sent 5 kilos of each, instead of .5 kilos.

No problem, it happens. There was a procedure. There was always a procedure. NanoPharm could never accept the extra pills back into inventory. The chain of custody was broken. Quality control rules dictated that all excess must be destroyed at the Institute.

Malcolm took one .5 kilo bottle of each drug and put them on his desk. He repacked the remaining pills in their boxes and sealed them with red tape that read: "WARNING! Pharmaceutical products. Destroy. DO NOT OPEN!"

He put the boxes on the to-be-burned shelf and got to work.

He opened a large fishing tackle box filled with Petri dishes, beakers, solvents and a digital scale. He ground five pills of Torpidan with a mortar and pestle. He put the powder in a petrie dish and added a few drops of distilled water.

Malcolm replaced his 3D glasses and headphones. Once more he felt himself floating, but around a different reef this time – with schools of tiny fish around a brain coral.

Let's see what we have here. He sniffed the petrie dish deeply. Hmm… very interesting… a soothing hops- like substance. But faint mixed only with water… perhaps a different solvent?

He crushed more pills and added a combination of liquids. This time the undersea world exploded with shapes and colors and connecting chains of molecules. His head swayed. He recognized a combination of carbon rings. He saw the precursors of tropane alkaloids – but incomplete – not enough to produce a psychotropic event. Not bad, he thought. No toxic level, a non-opiate relaxant. He saw several possible therapeutic uses.

Malcolm took off his headset, opened his laptop and searched for scientific confirmation about the identity of the molecules. In a few minutes he knew he was correct. He would follow up later with a detailed report. For now, he wrote out a brief "safe product" finding and emailed it to Grey Pearce, copying it to NanoPharm.

He repeated the procedure – first with water, then with other solvents – on the second drug, Epithet. He sniffed.

The reef and the water and the fish all changed colors slightly. Anthocyanins? Why have them?

He sniffed and felt his brain sharpen. He saw greater detail. His analytical focus increased. Curiously, his body felt relaxed, yet stimulated. He saw connecting phenolic compounds and waxy esters. He put the Petri dish down. Very nice, he thought, as he wrote out another "safe product" email.

The effects of Epithet were fading as he stood to put his kit away. But before it disappeared he had an inspiration: What about a combination of the two drugs?

He crushed up two pills of each drug, added water, sniff-tested it and from this determined the correct solvent. He crushed more pills, and added a drop or two of it. He sniffed.

He sat back in his chair. His head tilted back. His eyes closed. He had a twitchy smile on his face. He curled his wrists, and put his hands up to his chin. They moved like the legs of a dreaming dog.

His body went limp in his chair. His mind felt happy. His joints felt free. Tears welled up in his eyes. He cried a little. This could help Ms. Cup.

Malcolm mixed up a new batch, with different proportions, this time 70% Torpidan, 30% Epithet. He tried it, and his nano-body felt rejuvenated. His mind felt alert and inquisitive.

This is it! I know this will help her!

But... what if I switched the proportions? Would that be even better? He mixed again, this time with 70% Epithet.

He sniffed. His head felt like it was expanding. My god, he thought, this mixture creates a true tropane alkaloid/indole/phenethylamine blend.. I wonder which psychotropic drug it is?

He sniffed again. He saw before his eyes a slew of molecules, ones he had seen before, but a long time ago. He breathed again. He concentrated and the molecules became clearer. As his mind sharpened further, he remembered reading about a substance like this in an anthropology book on medicinal and religious mixtures.

He dropped his 3D glasses on the table and picked up the phone. Hours had gone by.

"Doyle," Malcolm said.

A groggy voice answered "...Yeah."

"Doyle, wake up."

"Huh? Malcolm? I just got to sleep. What time is it?"

"11 p.m. I want to come over."

"Not now... Lemme sleep... Not now."

"I'm coming over, right now," said Malcolm, and he hung up.

On his way out, Malcolm grabbed a bag of empty gelatin capsules and a capsule-filling device. He picked up the boxes of Torpidan and Epithet from the to-be-burned shelf and locked the door behind him.

CHAPTER 16

Doyle was deep asleep and dreaming. In the dream, he was trying to find a fancy restaurant where he had once worked for a much-hated boss. *Why am I going back?* He wandered outdoors in Eugene, but it was strange and unfamiliar. He couldn't find the restaurant. It had moved.

Then the phone rang.

"Doyle, wake up."

Still caught in the dream, Doyle at first thought he was hearing his hated ex-boss. *He found me!*

The dream evaporated. It was Malcolm... what? Ms. Cup...

"I'm coming over right now," said Malcolm. He hung up.

What the fuck?

Doyle put on his bathrobe, heated a cup of yesterday's coffee in the microwave, and sat on the living room couch in a stupor. The room was simply furnished but clean, filled with an assembly of matching thrift store furniture. A couple of soothing abstract paintings stared at each other across a hardwood floor, covered with an imitation Persian rug. By the window, a small table was crowded with handwritten music and lyrics, a laptop, a drum machine and a synthesizer. On a music stand, more music, next to a battered electric guitar covered with stickers.

Doyle put his feet up on his glass-top coffee table. A few years ago he would have had to move a bong and empty beer bottles to do so, but now he rested them on Rolling Stone magazines, neatly displayed next to a National Geographic coffee-table book on African travel. He took a swig of coffee and winced, remembering last night's threat by Laguna. *What will I* do? Why the fuck did I tell Benny? I got nothing. I'm going to jail.

He thought back to that night in the parking lot, spread-eagled and handcuffed against the hood of Laguna's Camaro.

"You're my bitch now," Laguna had said. He had dangled the evidence bag with two fingers. "Dutchie the snitch, I'll make sure your cell mates at Sheridan know all about you. Get ready to suck a mile of cock."

So it began. Doyle snitched. He felt worse each time. Now he was out of information. He pictured himself in an orange jumpsuit, eating overcooked, gray food. He pictured himself sitting on a toilet in plain view of indifferent guards and homicidal maniacs blowing him kisses. He shuddered and turned on the TV.

The doorbell rang. He turned it off again. Doyle took a deep breath, let it out and opened the door. Malcolm was balancing two large boxes in his arms. He couldn't see around them or over them.

"Uh, Malcolm. I gotta get back to sleep. Can we talk about…?"

"Let me in, Doyle." Malcolm pushed into the room. Doyle sighed and stepped aside.

Malcolm set the boxes down on the kitchen counter. He took off his backpack. He took out a heavy mortar, a pestle, and another device.

"What's going on?"

Malcolm ignored him. He counted out pills from each bottle and put them in the mortar. He opened a different big bottle, and added other pills.

"Here, Doyle, crush these pills to powder. Like this." Malcolm started crushing the pills. He handed the pestle to Doyle. "I'll get the capsule filler set up." Doyle dutifully began crushing. "OK, but... why am I doing this?"

"This formula will help Ms. Cup's arthritis. It's perfect to release her joints, to open them up." Malcolm held his hands up and opened them apart.

Doyle knew it was useless to argue. He continued crushing pills. When they were powder, Malcolm put the powder in a stainless steel bowl he'd found in Doyle's cupboard.

"Now count 20 pills of Torpidan and five of Epithet together, and crush them," said Malcolm.

Such was Malcolm's urgency that Doyle had counted the pills and begun crushing them before his intellect had time to kick in. "What are they?" he asked belatedly.

"Second-use pharmaceuticals. Both of these drugs sold poorly, didn't work well in their first release to the public, so NanoPharm hired the Institute to create new diseases to match them with."

"You stole these pills?"

"No. No. No. They're an over-shipment. It's no problem, it's part of my job to get rid of them." Malcolm filled capsules and put them in a bag. Doyle crushed more pills.

Soon they had hundreds of capsules.

"That's plenty, more than she'll need for years," said Malcolm. He picked up one capsule. He sat down heavily on the couch. Doyle sat at the breakfast bar and watched.

Malcolm opened the capsule, took a deep sniff and sat back. His head tilted back and his eyes closed. He had a twitchy smile on his face. He curled his wrists, and put his hands up to his chin. They moved under his chin like the legs of a dreaming dog.

Doyle knew these gestures well. He had seen Malcolm do this for many years; he called it Malcolm's molecular dream. If Malcolm spoke from this altered state, his words would come from a deep and important place.

"… Safe, even used every day. Yes, bad stress eats hormones. Release bad stress, and she will get flooded with natural hormones… her body will be repopulated with natural hormones. Similar to some of the effects of Xiao Yao Wan. It softens. It moves energy… pillowy… youthful… not habit forming… strongly euphoric."

Malcolm slowly brought his head down. His eyes were still closed. He took a breath. He let out a breath. He opened his eyes and looked at Doyle.

"It's funny," said Malcolm.

"What's funny?"

"This mixture. Either of these drugs is barely therapeutic by itself, but put them together and they will work great."

He looked thoughtful. "If you mix it differently, it makes a completely different compound, with a completely different effect. If you mix them in opposite proportions, it becomes an unusual psychotropic drug, similar to some of the plant combinations used by shamans in the Amazon."

Doyle suddenly was fully awake. "Is it dangerous?"

"No. That's what's so great. There is no overdose. It shuts itself off. It isn't habit-forming either. It crosses the blood-brain barrier, but doesn't over stimulate or exhaust the area that produces endorphins. But Ms. Cup doesn't need something that strong."

Malcolm got up. He filled zip-lock bags with capsules. "I'm going to see her right now. Want to come?"

"Uh, no thanks, Malcolm. You go. Give her a hug from me."

"Please throw out the rest of the pills. Just seal the boxes and toss everything in the dumpster. I'll pick up the equipment in the next few days."

"Sure. But Malcolm, it's almost one in the morning."

Malcolm, ignoring him, left. Doyle got up and watched him jog down the dark street.

Doyle felt wide awake. He wasn't tired at all.

He counted pills and crushed them, using the Ms. Cup formula. When he had a large zip-lock bag full, he put a couple of handfuls in a smaller bag – the bag for Victor Laguna.

He opened the bottles again. He counted out more pills – this time reversing the proportions. He crushed pills and filled capsules with the psychotropic formula. Soon he had hundreds and hundreds of capsules in a large bag. He put the remaining Epithet and Torpidan into his closet and turned off the lights. He fell into bed and instantly fell asleep.

It was late afternoon when he woke. Fortunately, Sunday was his day off. He got dressed and made himself coffee and an avocado and cheese omelet.

He pulled out the bag of psychotropic capsules and opened it.

He looked inside the bag of capsules and thought: A new psychotropic drug with no overdose potential?

Should I?

He took a single capsule in his fingers, and held it up to his eyes.

Here's to science.

He tossed it into his mouth.

CHAPTER 17

Doyle swallowed the capsule and washed it down with some water and a squeeze of lemon. He strummed his guitar idly.

He lit a candle and shut off the overhead light. A small table lamp provided a warm and comfortable view of his kitchen table/desk and the notebook before him. He gathered his creative tools: pens and pencils, music pad and drawing pad.

Then it began.

From the corner of his eye, he saw something shimmer: a small stuffed chair. It seemed to call him. He put down his guitar and exchanged his kitchen chair for the cushier, small easy chair. He sank into it. It was like an affectionate hug from a friend.

He sighed happily and picked up his guitar again. He strummed a chord and the blue pen moved on the table, all by itself. Doyle smiled and put the pen on top of the pad before him. It was an invitation of the spirit. The room was glowing with prismatic colors. It made him feel love overflowing. For a moment he was overwhelmed and his eyes moistened.

He looked at the pad and saw that he had written a verse.

"When my love is strong
and my heart is full
when there's nothing wrong
the magnetic pull.
From deep inside you now
I can feel your love
like a homing dove,
a ship's guided prow.
You're calling from the stars
Beyond the planets, and Mars

What is any man worth?
What are we doing on earth?"

When he next looked at his desk, he discovered he had penned twenty songs. He spent the next hour writing down all the notations required to re-create them. Some of them used chord inversions he had never tried before. Some seemed to require illustrations, so he drew little curly drawings in the margins, birds and suns and things that he wasn't quite sure what they were.

When dawn arrived, he watched the light change the color of the grass on the hill, from black to navy blue to dark green to an almost overwhelming bright green.. He got up from his cozy chair and took a shower, as hot as his plumbing would allow. His skin was bright red. The sound of the water plashing in the tub gave way to a melody, which gave him a word: bright.

Continuing to hum, he went to his electric keyboard. In a minute he had written another song: "This Bright Morning." He put on his shoes and left.

As he was closing the door, he saw that the breeze from the doorway had blown out his candle. He felt connected to the world in little and great things.

Alone, Doyle wandered the empty streets and felt the cool air pass through him. The early morning light was soft and tentative. It was as if the sun was being gentle to the streets.

He passed a restaurant that had a three-foot bag of rolls leaning against its front door. He reached into the bag and took two rolls. He replaced them with a $5 bill, the only money he was carrying.

He strolled the streets watching his neighborhood come to life. When day had fully begun, he walked back home and ate fresh rolls, orange marmalade and coffee. Feeling sleepy, he headed toward his bed and only then noticed the top of his desk. He'd completely forgotten: before him lay twenty complete songs, including words, chords, comments and in some cases drawings. He reviewed them each. They all seemed good. He wanted to sing them to Fawn.

He got to work early that day. He brought his guitar, a pad, and his pens, as well as a baggie full of Ms. Cup's pills in case Victor came in again. When Benny arrived, Doyle had been on his cell phone for hours, telling Fawn his poetical dreams and his love for her. He wanted to bring her with him wherever he went. He wanted to have Fawn in his breast pocket so he could touch her smile.

"My battery's starting to beep. I guess it's time to get off the phone." They exchanged I love you's in a way that felt authentic enough to carry each of them through the day.

CHAPTER 18

When Benny sauntered into The Nexus, Doyle was on his cell phone. They nodded to each other and Doyle continued to talk. Benny went to his locker to change his clothes, listening as hard as he could. He knew it was Fawn on the line because Doyle's voice was soft and his eyes were tender.

Benny unlocked his locker. He pulled the phone from his shirt pocket and took off his shirt, pulling a clean one off the locker shelf. Into the pocket of the clean shirt went the phone, newly equipped with gadgetry that he'd just purchased: his new toy allowed him to access five remote cameras, including audio. He looked at the sixth and final camera, with its state-of-the-art audio, sitting innocently in his ultra-secure locker. He'd considered placing it in the ladies' room, but that wasn't his style. Bodies didn't turn Benny on; interactions did. He wanted to know everything.

Benny closed his locker and spun the dial on its combination lock for extra security. Grabbing a cup of coffee, he made his way into the bar. It was empty, so he sat at the bar and watched Doyle work.

Doyle had spent the day re-arranging the liquor according to the flow of what was used most, rather than the haphazard arrangement left by his predecessor. It was something he had wanted to do for a long time but had always felt too lazy to tackle.

Benny's eyebrows went up to his hairline. "We are industrious today, aren't we?"

"Yes, we are. We are moving everything in the right direction today."

"Well! We are also quite chipper, aren't we?" Benny realized what must be going on. "How are you doing with Fawn?"

"Great," said Doyle, grinning.

"That's it – just great? C'mon, don't leave me hanging."

Doyle found the intensity of Benny's examination a little off-putting. What does he really want? Why is he asking all these questions? He thought about it for a moment. That's just what Benny does, I guess. He asks questions.

"So, Benny, what if I were to tell you I was deeply connected to Fawn and my feelings for her are unlike any I've ever had for anyone in my entire life?"

Benny nodded in satisfaction. "Good for you, Dutchie. I'm happy for you. Like that old song 'Blue skies shining on me', you know that one?"

"Yeah, I know that one."

Benny's eyes over the edge of his cup as he sipped his coffee didn't reflect his happy tone, Doyle noticed. He saw deep sadness, mixed with anger, perhaps even rage. Then the goading questions began again.

"So, Doyle, you getting any?"

On any other day Doyle would take the bait and spar with Benny, returning his invasive questions with a good-natured remark of his own. Today was different.

"What is it, Benny? It's loneliness, isn't it? You kid around a lot, but you really just want to make contact." His guess had scored: Benny's eyes welled up. Doyle felt a rush of concern.

The moment of vulnerability disappeared from Benny's face, replaced immediately with the usual cynical smirk. "We all have our problems, don't we, Dutchie? Right now mine is having some lunch. How about a sandwich?"

"Sure, Benny. Ham on rye for me. We have fifteen minutes till opening, so make it quick."

CHAPTER 19

Victor Laguna's Camaro pulled into the Nexus parking lot in the very early evening. He was about to roust a young couple sitting in a parked car, just for kicks: maybe there'd be drugs, or if he was really lucky a quick blow job from an intimidated girlfriend. Then he noticed Croakie's funeral car pulling in at the other end of the lot.

Victor bounded over to the car like a child greeting his dad at the front door. Croakie unfolded his tall frame from the huge car, followed closely by the Swede and the Greek deli man.

"This is it, Victor. I want you to take care of Fawn Fallingsnow. She put up that video on the Internet and we need for her to take it down and to denounce it publicly as a fraud. I don't care what you have to do to get her to do it, but if you don't, your Camaro is in the junkyard and you're looking for a new job. Do I make myself clear?"

"Sure, Art, don't I always take care of you? I'll fix it."

Art handed him a card with Fawn's address on it. "Fuck this up, Victor, and it's all over. You fucked up before, and we all know about that." The Swede and the Greek nodded sycophantically. "But if you fuck up this time, we're going down and taking you with us. No more cash flow, no more blowjob shakedowns. It goes away, all of it. You got me?" Spittle sprayed out onto Victor's shirt.

"Don't worry, I'll take care of it."

"Not like you took care of those kids in Springfield, Victor! You owe us one, Mr. Camaro. You break it, you pay." Croakie shook his raised index finger in Victor's face and turned to go.

"So you guys having dinner, or what? I'll be in in a minute, save me a seat."

79

"No Victor, you're not having dinner with us. We pay you to do work for us. We pay you to ride around in your stupid car. We don't pay you to be our buddy, 'cause you're not. You want dinner, you go sit somewhere else." Croakie and friends turned and went in, leaving Victor standing alone, wiping the spittle off his tie. Hurt and angry, but obedient, Victor waited several minutes before he went into the Nexus, and sat alone at the bar, fuming with humiliation. In the mirror he saw Croakie's gang sitting with a pitcher of beer, chatting and laughing. It made his collar feel tight and his face feel hot.

Down at the other end of the bar, Doyle had his head down washing glassware, and had missed the whole thing. Laguna got up and walked over. He looked left and right.

He grabbed his shirt lapels and adjusted them by lifting and lowering them several times.

He leaned in close.

He jutted his chin.

He cocked his head.

He poked his chin forward, two or three times, without saying a word.

Doyle watched him, a tired look of resignation on his face. "So, Victor, how's it going?"

"Don't bullshit me, Doyle. You know why I'm here. And you better have something for me."

"Oh sure, Vic. Don't worry, I got something for you. Sit down, have a drink. The usual?" Victor didn't calm down. His anger from the parking lot was still boiling, the steam needed an escape route, and Doyle was the closest outlet. "You wanna go to prison, pal? Is that it?"

"Calm down, Vic. I have something for you. I think you'll like it. I got it off someone who was passing through town with one of the bands. He gave me a bag of something new. Follow me."

Doyle caught Benny's eye and, with a gesture, asked him to cover the bar while he dealt with Victor. From behind the bar, Benny watched carefully as Victor followed Doyle into the break area/changing room/storage room. Doyle went to his guitar case and pulled out a bag of the non-psychotropic Ms. Cup formula and handed them to Victor.

"This is it, Victor. You can take my name off the wall. You can throw away that LSD you have. We are done. These pills are the hottest thing happening. These will be sweeping the country and you're way ahead of the curve. You'll be the officer who discovers them. It'll make your career."

"What are they?"

In a sudden panic, Doyle realized he had no name for the capsules. He looked frantically around the room and his eye fell on a bottle of Lubriderm by the sink.

"They're called Lubridone. Everyone calls them Lubers."

"Lubridone, Lubers." Victor muttered, fingering the bag with growing excitement. He stuffed the bag in his pocket.

Benny, who had seen the whole transaction in the bar mirror, asked the cook to make Victor's favorite sandwich. He stuck his head into the break room. "I have a sandwich for you at the bar, your usual. Did you want a beer with that?"

Laguna considered the offer. Now that his anger was dissipating in the prickling sense of excitement of a possible career advancement, he realized that he was starving. "A sandwich, huh? Sure, why not? And a Bud."

Benny set the pickled egg sandwich and the thin foamy brew in front of him. "Enjoy, Vic."

CHAPTER 20

His heart pounding, Benny slipped out the back door of the Nexus. He didn't have much time. The Camaro gleamed in the circle of light under a streetlamp, so visual privacy was not an option. On the other hand, the parking lot was empty and nobody seemed to be around on mostly residential Friendly Street.

He set his backpack on the asphalt beside the Camaro. He dropped to the ground, and pulled himself completely under the car, his nose inches from the oil drain. With one hand he pulled the ceramic induction power tap from his backpack, and clipped it onto the main power wire from the battery to the starter.

From the power tap he strung four feet of wire to a magnetic-backed receiver, transmitter, recording and GPS unit, then attached the electronics to the undercarriage. The wire would act as an antenna, giving Benny the ability to track this car anywhere in an eighty-square-mile radius.

This took thirty seconds, but it seemed a lot longer. His forehead was dripping sweat. Then, he heard the squeak that meant the door to the Nexus was opening. If it was Laguna, Benny was sunk.

He peeked out of the darkness under the car and saw a wedge of light as a young couple entered the bar. The parking lot got quiet again. He took a deep breath and pulled himself back out from under the car.

Now for the dangerous part.

He tried the front door of the car. It was unlocked! He slid onto the front seat and ducked down. From his bag he took a cordless drill. He drilled a tiny hole in the edge of the interior dome light.

He put away the drill and took out a tiny, wide-angle camera and microphone, disguised as a screw. He screwed it into the hole. He slipped out of the car, closed the door quietly and headed back to work.

The door opened as he reached for it. Laguna walked out. The cop nodded curtly to Benny.

To Benny, Victor looked preoccupied. I wonder what he's thinking about? I wonder where he's going?

CHAPTER 21

By the time Doyle got to Fawn's house, the day had melted away; he felt untroubled and serene. He and Fawn sat together in an old porch swing on her front porch. Rusty chains creaked. Macrouder, the last of the Greenwerks crowd that had joined them for a potluck dinner, sat quietly in a lawn chair next to them; everyone else had left, Clive was in his crib asleep, the dishes could wait for later. They sat in the dark looking at the quiet street.

Doyle daydreamed. He was future-Doyle, sitting right here, enjoying year after year on a porch swing, with his arm around a pretty blond girl in a sundress, who was leaning her head on his shoulder, with her bare legs tucked under her. She loved him.

For the first time in his life Doyle felt completely content. A kind of lucidity suffused him: his emotions, his sensuality, his intellect and his creative mind were synchronized at last. He was thinking rationally, welcoming his emotions thoroughly, and reveling in creative joy. The capsule had been much more than just a high; he felt transformed. And tonight he was in love.

He saw the selfishness of his past, and he let it go. I could love you forever, Fawn.

Macrouder drank the last of the red wine from his glass. "Fawn, I finally read that VertBild material you gave me last month."

"Last month? More like last year."

"Sorry about that. I've been busy."

"Well, what did you think?"

"It's awesome. I want to be part of it."

"I knew you would," she said. "That's why I signed on with them. VertBild is perfect for Eugene, if only I could get a fair hearing. But I can't. I can't get past the old boys' club of developers that run the city. All the old companies get the best building projects, they never use recycled materials or emerging technologies, and they take all the available money for publicly funded projects."

"You get a commission, right?" asked Macrouder.

"Yeah, plus a small base salary. It's been slow, though – a small sale in Seattle, one in Portland, but nothing in Eugene. And it's perfect for here."

"VertBild's concept is great for remodeling homes or building new homes," said Macrouder. "I love the way they integrate new green technologies – the recycled construction materials, the local manufacturing, the advanced eco-technology products... it's fantastic. And it's all licensed and made in America."

Fawn lifted her head off Doyle's shoulder. "Wait till you see the pamphlet I got today about their new investment programs. It's revolutionary. You can invest by buying a VertBild remodeled house, or remodeling your own house, or buying a new VertBild house. You can invest in a real estate investment trust featuring joint home ownership, or you can invest directly in the parent company by buying stock. The goal is to create communities of VertBild homes, with central administration to keep the occupants connected to each other and to social services, if necessary. VertBild landlords have to commit to finding creative ways to keep tenants in their rentals if the tenants hit hard times."

"I like the bartering system, and the sustainable garden plots, too." said Macrouder. "Like I said, I believe in it. If only we could sell it to the city."

Doyle had an idea. "What if Fawn could speak about it at the Free LeBron concert?"

"Perfect," said Macrouder. "You can have time after the Cosmic Bee's first set." Fawn smiled happily.

"So it's still on for next weekend?" asked Doyle.

"So far," said Macrouder. "Everything was set up for a downtown, permit, insurance and everything. Then at the last minute, somebody higher up – probably Croakie – squelched it. I tried to get into the Saturday Market stage, but no dice. Finally, we got space on campus, and so far, so good."

Macrouder stood. "Well, that's set, then... but I'm beat. I'm headed for home. Wonderful dinner, Fawn." He bent down and gave her a kiss on the cheek, and high-fived Doyle.

He was heading down the stairs when he heard Doyle's voice "Wait a minute."

Macrouder turned. "Yeah?"

"I had this crazy idea for raising money for LeBron's bail."

"Tell me. We need all the ideas and money we can get."

Doyle took in a deep breath. He didn't know how this would play. "It's kind of risky, and not too legal."

Macrouder didn't say anything. Fawn sat up in the swing.

"I was given a large quantity of a very benign psychoactive drug. It's both wild and mild, and brand new. There's no overdose possibility. It's fun. It's creative. I've taken it. It's amazing. It's unique. Not so much of a high, it's more of a gateway to a creative state of being. It's transformational and healing." Doyle took a baggie out of his pocket and handed it to Macrouder. "Here's a couple of capsules, for two people. If you don't want them, throw them away."

Macrouder paused for a moment, then nodded and tucked the baggie into his pocket. "OK," he said. "Goodnight, Fawn." They waited as his footsteps echoed down the street.

Fawn got up and went inside the house. She came back out with a sweater. She didn't rejoin Doyle in the porch swing, but sat on the lawn chair, her arms folded across her chest. Uh-oh.

"You OK?" he asked.

"You don't know what you're doing."

"What?"

"Getting involved with Santos and Brigger – selling drugs. LeBron can handle his time in jail, but what about the seventh-graders who are going to take your dope. Are you OK with that?"

"Wait. Who's Santos? Who's Brigger?"

"The drug dealers who are going to sell your dope – the ones Macrouder would use. Macrouder doesn't sell drugs, barely takes any as far as I know. But there's lots of people at Greenwerks who are big-time into drugs."

"I'll tell Macrouder no kids, only adults."

"Oh, well, why didn't you say so? That makes it all so much better. I feel so relieved."

"Look, Fawn..."

"I'm not a puritan, Dutch. I'm not against all drug use, but I'm a mother and I don't want kids taking drugs." Staring into the distance, Fawn looked like a woman on a train of strangers, pulling away from the station.

They sat silently on the porch. The creaky porch swing was the only sound.

He waited to see if she would say something. She didn't.

After a long quiet while, he said, "I think I'll go home." She turned to him. He couldn't read her expression. He walked over to give her a kiss. She waited till he was near, then leaned slightly forward and gave him a dry, quick kiss on the lips.

At least it wasn't a peck on the cheek, he thought, as he walked back home in the dark.

CHAPTER 22

Fawn sat in the dark. She felt drained and tired and disappointed.

She heard footsteps approaching and stood up from her porch chair. Is it Doyle coming back for, a real kiss?

She reached inside the open door and flipped on the porch light. A man stepped in close. He held out a card: "Victor Laguna, Detective, Eugene Police Department."

"Fawn, I need a few words with you, this is a police matter. Please come with me to the car."

"What is this about? My son's upstairs sleeping. I don't want to leave him there."

"It will only be a minute, ma'am. Please step into the cruiser."

"That's not a police car."

"Yes, Ma'am, it is. I'm a detective."

"Well, I..."

"I must insist that you come with me."

Fawn turned to look upstairs. The house was silent. No chance of her son waking up in a few minutes. She nodded and followed him.

Laguna opened the passenger door of the Camaro and Fawn got in. Laguna got into the driver's seat and let out a long sigh.

Sitting in the dark in front of his computer screen, Benny saw the lights come on inside Laguna's car. He recognized Fawn.

"What the fuck?"

"It has come to our attention that certain of your behaviors cannot continue." Laguna spoke in a deep monotone. To Benny, the night-vision camera gave the faces ghoulish, green features.

He saw fear cross Fawn's face.. "What are you talking about, officer?" she asked.

"You made a video that is doctored and that does not tell the truth. You must remove it from the Internet and all media immediately, and post a disclaimer saying it was false. It's over. Do you understand me?"

"Well, you know what, Officer Lasagna? That's not gonna happen. It's too late. Everyone already knows the truth." Fawn reached for the door handle, but froze when she felt Laguna's meaty hand on her arm.

"You're not going anywhere. Bad things can happen to you. Painful things."

"I'm getting out of this car and you can't stop me." Fawn yanked her arm away..

"No, you're not. Just think about this. You've been seen neglecting your son." Benny saw Fawn's eyes widen in sudden fear. "You don't want him taken from you, do you? Foster homes can be tough, you know. Getting your kid back can take months or even years, and who knows what could happen to him in the meantime? Think about what I'm saying."

Benny's heart pounded.

"But, you know, we probably don't even need to go there." Laguna opened his pants. He pulled out his cola-can-wide and fully erect member. "You see this, bitch? You see how fat this thing is? It's gonna go right up your ass and straight down your throat. You're gonna choke on it, and your ass is gonna bleed. And I'm gonna come back again and again. You hear me? You understand?"

"That's pathetic. Is that how desperate you are, that you have to rape women to get off?" Oops, that was a little too close to home, thought Benny, who had known Laguna for years. And sure enough, the cop gasped in rage. He tried to put Fawn's hand on his dick. She struggled, but he easily held her in place, moving his hips so that her hand was rubbing him.

Benny's breathing was rapid now. He felt a knot in his stomach. Did I see her hand touch him? Is she really touching him? Holy shit, she might be rubbing him. I've heard that some women like it rough. Could she be turned on?

The intimacy, the interaction, was there. Benny was aroused. He touched himself. She wants him, she wants him, oh God she wants him.

But then Laguna suddenly let go of Fawn's hand. She lunged for the door and launched sideways out of the car, falling hard on the sidewalk. Crying, she bolted for the house.

"You'll pay for this, bitch. It's not over. You don't get the video off the air, your ass is mine," Laguna shouted, his cruel expression caught clearly in the ghoulish green light.

I guess she wasn't turned on. I better call Doyle.

CHAPTER 23

But somehow, Benny didn't call Doyle, not right away. He played and replayed the part of the recording where Fawn's soft hand touched Laguna's freakish dick. There it is. See, she's moving her hand on her own. He trained her to want him. There it is. Her fingers are touching him.

Benny played it over and over again, his own hand moving faster and faster on his own penis, until at last he erupted. He collapsed backwards onto his bed. The energy conservation routine on his monitor kicked in and left the room in blackness. His thoughts raced.

How can I tell Doyle about this? I can't tell him. Then he'll know about the surveillance. But I think she touched him, and he's a cop. Holy shit. How can I just let this happen?... Eventually, though, the aftermath of his orgasm caught up to him, and he fell asleep.

When he woke up the next morning, Benny realized he had evidence that could put a cop away for a long time. He showered his sticky body, still thinking.

He couldn't tell Doyle, not now, not yet.

I want to see more.

CHAPTER 24

The next night after work, Benny stayed up late again to eavesdrop on Laguna. Mostly he heard ordinary police business, but late in the evening he noticed a change. This can't be police business – the police radio is off.

The tiny camera in the ceiling of Laguna's Camaro was in night-vision mode. In his bedroom, Benny adjusted the image on his screen. He filtered out the white light of oncoming headlights, giving him a clear view of the zombie-green side of Laguna's face as he drove.

Where's he going?

Benny split his computer screen in half vertically. On the right side, he pulled up a GPS map of Eugene. A pulsing red dot showed the location of the Camaro. A crawl of words at the bottom of the screen changed every few seconds, showing the street address of the car as it moved west.

What's he doing in the industrial district?

The pulsing red dot stopped. Benny's speakers went silent as the motor shut off.

Laguna sat in the dark.

Stakeout? Benny copied the street address into a public records database. Croakie Funeral Homes, LLC. What the...?He adjusted the camera to maximum wide angle view: A plain steel-sided industrial building with rollup doors all along the side and signs of various sizes over each door. Funeral home warehouse.

Laguna pulled out a cell phone. Benny turned up the volume.

"So where is everybody? I'm here, now..." Laguna's voice came through the speakers as clearly as if he were standing in Benny's bedroom.

"Whattya mean tomorrow? I thought Zebra Club was tonight..."

Zebra Club?

"Tomorrow, then. Hey... On that other thing, good news. I took care of Fawn what's-her-name for you. I showed her the big can. I'll go back and show her some more if you need me... or maybe even if you don't. I almost got a hand job from her." Laguna chuckled. Benny heard a second laugh, tinny-sounding, from Laguna's phone. Who's he talking to?

"Look, I gotta go. I'll see you tomorrow night. Make sure you bring Beatrice... I'm gonna fuck her for you and everyone can watch." A gleam of green shadows illuminated Laguna's wolfish smile.

"So, Mr. Mayor, say goodnight to Mrs. Mayor. And don't you lose a moment's sleep over that Fawn bitch, she's taken care of." Laguna snapped his phone shut and turned the key to bring the Camaro roaring to life.

Benny switched off the audio and sat back in his chair, stunned.

Croakie. That fucker ordered Laguna to go after Fawn.

Benny entered "Croakie" into an Internet database. Dozens of parcels of real estate popped up. Several were jointly owned by Arthur J. Croakie and Beatrice P. Croakie, husband and wife.

Early the next morning Benny walked over to his closet and slid back one side. Pondering, he flipped through an assortment of uniforms. "Water meter reader? Electric? Pest control? City building inspector? Ah, yes, that's it -- fire safety." Benny pulled out a handsome uniform cleverly cobbled together from a dark blue thrift-store jacket with a few sewn-on patches. From the shelf above, he took down a conductor's hat with a badge affixed to its front. He added the blue Salvation Army pants with the stripe down the side, plus the clipboard that is the basic disguise for any investigator, and knew that in this rig even an actual fire inspector wouldn't recognize him as a civilian.

Ten minutes later, clipboard in hand, he knocked on the door of Croakie's warehouse. A middle-aged woman dressed in ill-fitting trousers, a polo shirt and Crocs answered. "I'm sorry to have to tell you this, but my superiors are asking for a complete rundown on this building, and I'm going to have to go through it with a fine-toothed comb. You and any other employees should probably just take a break for the next two hours, get some lunch or something."

"Yes, officer. Is there any danger?"

"No, ma'am. It's a routine annual inspection that slipped through the cracks somehow, and now I have to get it done today or state penalties will be assessed. Sorry for the inconvenience."

"Oh, that's all right, it's a slow day. I'll call the back and get everyone out. They're just sweeping up anyhow." She said a few words into a phone receiver, and two employees gleefully marched out the front door a few minutes later.

"I'll call you as soon as I'm done," said Benny, looking at his wristwatch and making a note on his clipboard.

When he was sure they were gone, Benny got to work. Moving quickly but carefully, he retrieved his kit from the trunk and began looking around. Almost immediately, he found what he was looking for: a huge area of the warehouse decorated like the den in an affluent suburban home. Fifty people could easily sit in the plush padded room, decorated with luxuriously thick carpets, giant pillows, sofas and chairs.

Within an hour, Benny installed strategic audio/video cameras covering every square inch of the space. From his car he tested each one on his portable monitor. It took a while to adjust and test them to perfection, but Benny was nothing if not a perfectionist. He picked up the phone.

"Your building is safe, ma'am. You can return to work now. Thank you for your time."

"That's it?"

"Yes, ma'am, that's it."

CHAPTER 25

Laguna had ignored his wife Marta for months, maybe years. He preferred furtive power sex with hookers.

Marta, ever hopeful, had done all she could to attract him. She restricted her diet and danced in front of the TV every morning. Although she'd once been an up-and-coming junior manager in a successful financial management firm, Victor had prohibited her from working years before – "nobody's ever gonna say I can't take care of my woman." Occasionally she met her sister for coffee, and she volunteered at the community center, but mostly she spent her day grooming herself in the hopes that Victor would find her beautiful enough.

Marta's efforts had made her thin and fashionable and strong, but over the years of working at her model-like dimensions, she had drained away the suppleness that comes with adequate nourishment; her muscles looked sinewy and her overly tanned skin was thin and crinkly. Her hard work kept her in her high school dress size, but gave her the jerky-like look that haunts the gated compounds of Florida. Even if she'd been as lush as the young Monroe, nothing would have brought Victor back into her bed, but, horny and lonely, she never gave up trying. They'd had a hot sex life once and she was sure that there must be a formula to get it back again.

Food, maybe? "What would you like for dinner, dear? How about a juicy steak? With salad and potatoes? Or how about something special, baby, like empanadas?"

"Ah, not yet, maybe later." He puttered in the kitchen, fixing himself a drink, irritated, rejecting her offer to do it for him. "Henry sleeping?"

"He went to sleep about twenty minutes ago." Her eyebrows rose hopefully.

Ignoring her, Victor took the bag of pills from his jacket and set them on the counter.

"What are those, Victor? Drugs, with Henry in the house?"

"Just calm down, willya? it's a new sex pill we're gonna try."

Marta would have yipped and stood on her back legs and turned circles if she could. Instead, she smiled tremulously, her eyes riveted on the baggie.

After taking out two capsules and setting them on a plate, Victor sealed the bag and put it away in the cabinet. He handed her a pill and kept one for himself. Her heart beating frantically, she poured them each a tumbler of juice. They clinked glasses. "Bottoms up," she said.

"We can do it that way too," he said, and grinned.

Victor washed and undressed, taking his time, sipping his juice. By the time he sat on the edge of the bed, Marta was more than ready for him. Her silk robe loose in front so her enhanced breasts peeked out, she assumed her usual position on her knees before him.

"No, not like that, not this time. Just relax and let the pill go to work." She nodded and stretched out stiffly on her side of the bed, too nervous to read or watch TV.

Twenty minutes later, they were starting to feel their Lubers. To Marta, it felt like a small earthquake making every nerve in her body quiver, accompanied by a rich flow of hormones unlike anything she'd felt since high school. Her senses were nearly overloaded – every smell became a signal that suggested mating season had arrived, every fluid that could secrete was seeping. Looking at Victor, she could see it was affecting him too: his nostrils were flared and his muscles twitched, the long-pastured bull catching a whiff of a female in her season.

"Want some music, babe?"

She nodded.

They danced in the living room. Her eyes shone romantically, as in love with him as she'd ever been, full of desire and affection.

They kissed. They hugged. He led her down the hall, hand-in-hand.

The night lasted for years or for moments, she couldn't decide. She and Vic could not stop touching and exploring each other's bodies. Vic's skin was a dark, furry, inviting tableau and her hands couldn't leave it. She came again and again, from the simplest touch, each orgasm carrying her higher, tirelessly ecstatic. Finally, exhausted, they fell asleep in each other's arms as the dawn started to lighten the sky that peeked between their drawn curtains.

At 6:30 A.M., Marta slid out of bed to wake Henry for school. She fed him and got him out the door, making sure that Victor was not disturbed.

Victor was snoring quietly when she returned. She undressed and slipped back into bed beside her husband. She ached to press against him, to mingle with him until they were one indistinguishable being. Her hands trailed lightly over his chest and belly. He moaned, smiled, turned on his side away from her. She moved close, stroked his back, kissed his shoulder passionately. Victor groaned. Her body flattened against him, her erect nipples ground into his back. Victor whimpered and began to pant. Her hand roamed to his genitals and circled his penis with her soft fingers. He was already fully erect. Victor's hips pumped involuntarily into her grasp. Her hand went from his dick up to his chest, clasping him closely.

"Why'd you stop?" he protested.

"We had such a lovely night, didn't we, Vic? Just like old times."

"Yeah, it was great, hon. They're called Lubers. Great stuff, huh?" Victor pulled her on top of him and rubbed his beer-can-like penis against her. Her soreness from the previous night's love fest dissolved in yet another surge of desire; she couldn't get enough of him. He entered her and she rocked herself to wild orgasmic bliss, her knees beside his hips shaking with spasms of release.

Just imagine what it would feel like to shake down a crack whore while I'm on this stuff, Victor thought. He held back, letting the fantasy suspend him in lustful bliss. Keeping her for hours, maybe in the trunk of the Camaro. Take her out during

97

the day anytime I feel a little horny. In his mind he combed the streets, thinking about where to find her.

Marta's keening howl of pleasure didn't interrupt his train of thought. She smiled into his eyes, then collapsed onto his chest and stretched her light wiry body on top of him. Victor held her close as her breathing and heartbeat slowed. How quick can I get away with leaving?

"I gotta get to work, babe." Maybe down in the Whitaker neighborhood...

She made a token protest, but truly she was done, and the pill's effect was starting to wear off. He slid out from under her. "Love you, honey," she murmured, and curled up happily into the warm, sex-scented covers.

CHAPTER 26

Victor combed the alleys behind Sixth Avenue. It won't be long now. He popped another Lubridone. It would be at least twenty minutes before he started to feel the edgy sexy rush of it. Enough time to find just the right one.

The Camaro crept slowly through the rutted alley, its headlights picking out the shady hovels and the spaces between buildings where whores and the homeless sometimes could be found. He scanned every niche and doorway for the figure of an unfortunate woman desperate and awake, someone who could satisfy his demands. Four blocks later he saw a man and woman. Although they were in their twenties, they had the ruddy complexions of those who sleep outdoors; he knew the look. He pulled up.

"Hey, what are you two up to?"

They spun around panic-stricken. The man protectively put his arm around the woman. "We aren't doing anything wrong, dude. We're just walking along, minding our own business."

"I'm a cop, and I think you're loitering." He looked into their eyes; their pupils were nearly invisible. The woman had once been beautiful, but her pretty face was hidden under dirt, weather, and years of abuse. Heroin, then.

"Let's say we make a deal," said the man. "My lovely friend will do whatever you want her to for just a twenty-dollar bill.".

"I got a better deal," Laguna said evenly. "How about I arrest you and beat the shit out of you, and then I fuck your girlfriend? You like that deal?"

"C'mon buddy, let's be fair. She's really worth it." The woman was starting to look alarmed.

"Naah, I think we're gonna do it my way." Slamming the car door behind him, Laguna handcuffed the man to a post. "Get in the car, sister." The Luber was starting to kick in, and he didn't want to miss a minute of it.

She slid passively into the car and took off her clothes. He reached over and tossed them out the window. She started to say something, but then thought better of it and subsided.

"Get into the back seat." He climbed in beside her. He stared at her lovely body, not yet ravaged by heroin addiction. He lay down in the back seat and she went down on him with practiced smoothness. Her head bobbed.

What's wrong with this pill? It's not like it was with Marta. He was enjoying his blowjob, but nothing else – no rich sensual flow, no heady release. The Lubridone was not working and Victor didn't like that, but he'd held off on ejaculating into his wife and his balls were starting to ache badly.

Cursing, he grabbed her head and pushed it hard over his freakish cock. She struggled for breath, and her struggle pushed him over the edge. She gagged and began to cough. He watched her tearing eyes as he finished and wiped himself clean.

"Now get out of here." Victor stood, pulled up his pants and watched her pale body as she slipped from the car to gather her clothes and dress from the dirty pavement. He opened the garage door, began to drive away, then remembered and unlocked her friend.

Laguna backed out of the garage. For a moment he considered giving the pair a little money, but he was too angry at not getting his high.

CHAPTER 27

Doyle was walking home after working the lunch shift, enjoying the warm sun on his face and checking out garage sales along Friendly Street, when his cell phone rang.

"Amazing shit, dude, really amazing. Blockhead changed me." It was Macrouder.

"Blockhead?"

"That's the name Russell gave it. Kind of funny, right?"

"Blockhead." Doyle chuckled.

They talked about their experiences. The words Macrouder used to describe his trip were different from the ones Doyle would have chosen, but it was clear that the two men's experiences had been similar: a life-altering synthesis of body, mind and spirit.

"I'll take all you got. My friend says he can get $25 per capsule, easily. We can free LeBron. Thanks, man."

"Uh... yeah. Just one thing," said Doyle. "We can't let this get into the hands of kids."

Macrouder started laughing. "Fawn, huh? You walked into that one, man. I saw it coming a mile away."

"I've got to insist."

"Seriously, Doyle, don't worry, I wouldn't involve Santos or Brigger. I don't trust them for this one, even though they're volunteers. Fawn hates them. I don't know why she thinks I'd use them. Nah, I've got a couple of frat boys at the U of O who can handle it, that's the best I can do. And if you don't want to do it, I understand. But either way, can you spare a couple more for me?"

Doyle thought about it. He balanced out the options, the beneficial effects. He thought about Fawn.

He decided to take the chance.

"Come on over and get 'em."

CHAPTER 28

Benny sat in the security of his bedroom. The "do not enter" sign on his door was only that the first of the fail-safes ensuring that no one went into his room. The keyed door, the newly installed motion-activated camera, and the number-activated bolt on his metal door actually did a far better job, in Benny's opinion.

Benny was able to switch between three cameras installed in the metal walls of Croakie's warehouse. He was watching tape from the previous night. The audio track wasn't very useful, due to the loud music; the only conversations he could hear were from people within a couple of feet of one of the cameras.

Scanning the crowd, Benny recognized some people – some from the bar and other local venues, some from the papers. Even though they wore costumes, few had bothered to cover their faces. They want to know who's who, Benny thought. Only one man didn't wear a costume: Bill Dhey, the owner of NanoPharm, was wearing a well-cut Armani suit, sipping a martini, ignoring the raucous goings-on around him as he conversed seriously with a fat man wearing a leopard-skin cape. There was a knock on Benny's door. He checked the room monitor and listened for the special knock: one, two, one, two, three: code for "it's mom with food." The monitor showed a plate of spaghetti and meatballs, his favorite. He got up and let her in.

"Thanks, mom, that's my favorite." Long ago, Benny had convinced himself that he was helping his mother feel more useful in her later years by staying at home, keeping her company and allowing her to attend to all his needs. How sad she would feel if he moved out!

She pecked him absently on the cheek and went downstairs. He sat in front of a different screen and quickly reviewed input from other cameras he had set up throughout the neighborhood.

There's Mrs. Gill's house, Roto-Rooter again? That's quite often. Uh, huh, now I see. How many drain cleaners kiss their customers?

He leaned forward and jotted down the camera number and date when the evidence appeared.

If I wanted to, I'll bet I could make a few bucks from Mrs. Gill with these pictures. Then I could buy another monitor, or that great control module I saw on New Egg.

Nothing else was interesting today. He printed out stills of Mrs. Gill's infidelity and re-set the tapes to record anew. He finished eating his spaghetti quickly, as he was saving the Zebra Club video for dessert. Benny belched. Out the window, he saw his mom chatting with a neighbor.

"Where's my dessert, Ma?" he muttered to himself. Spaghetti and meatballs always came with a large bowl of chocolate pudding, she knew that. Benny didn't want to call out to his mom through the window; it would embarrass her. He could call her on the house phone and let it ring until she answered. Or he could trigger the house alarm and interrupt her unimportant chatter with the roar of the huge klaxon he had bolted to the outside wall of the kitchen. He paced his room contemplating his alternatives, then saw the neighbor waving and turning to leave.

"OK, OK," he reassured himself. "She's coming."

Holding the sauce-smeared spaghetti plate, he paced until he heard her steps. He pulled the door open. "Great food, mom. I loved it."

"OK," she said offhandedly. "Well, here's your dessert." She grabbed the plate and handed him a huge bowl of pudding with heavy cream poured on top.

"Thanks, mom."

He shut and bolted his door.

She turned and trudged downstairs for the seventh time that day. Dear Lord, please help my son to leave my house. Isn't it about time? She shook her small grey head.

CHAPTER 29

Benny finished the pudding and kicked off his shoes. He turned down the room lights and pulled off his pants and t-shirt. Illegal surveillance tapes were best viewed in underwear.

He clicked "play" and sat back. People wore odd costumes. Animal outfits with pointy or floppy ears, long tails and furry paws were attached to everyone; one or two were dressed as horses, with bridles, saddles and hooves that shone with the gleam of expensive leather and steel. The lights were bright throughout the warehouse except along the back wall.

A group of young women arrived dressed as puppies. All wore knee pads and fingerless gloves to protect their young flesh from the floor as they crawled on all fours throughout the night. He saw that their task was to service and prepare the celebrants by performing tasks that actual dogs are generally scolded and sent out of the room for doing.

"There's Bob from the hardware store," Benny whispered. "That must be his wife. A dog, a cat, a tiger, those two are ponies... not sure exactly what that one's supposed to be. Wow, look at her, never seen her before... what's under that trench coat? Is that a dog penis? God, look at it, all bright red and thin, it looks wet... sexy with those thigh-high boots and that tight leather top... oh, my...."

Benny's hands dropped to his lap as the little puppies kneeled before the penis-wielding woman, licking her legs, sucking the slim and greasy red penis. Benny was getting close to exploding when he noticed Victor entering the warehouse. Victor wore no costume. He pulled a bag of capsules out of his pocket. Woo hoo, here come the drugs!

Victor poured some capsules into a large bowl and set them on a small table near the door. Everyone crowded around the bowl and took one. The bowl emptied quickly as more people – a Dalmatian-jacketed woman, a beagle man, a plump middle-aged tigress – filed in. Benny recognized fewer people now.

Big Art Croakie entered with his entourage, the tall Swede and the Greek deli owner. Art's wife Beatrice wore floppy fake-fur spaniel ears, a flowing see-through dress and furry flip-flops. Benny fast-forwarded through the next twenty minutes of tape, all tame introductory stuff. Puppies were crawling and lapping, arrivals were greeting and groping. Something caught his eyes and he stopped.

"Will ya look at that!" The deli man had pinned down a young puppy who had been readying him. He was banging into her with all three hundred pounds of his fleshy body, when the doggy dominatrix approached from the rear and began spanking his plump buttocks. Her gloved fingers wandered and caressed and he began to pump harder. She moved her hips behind him and with one sharp thrust entered him with her shiny, narrow dog penis. She pounded him hard. Her "paws," their latex sheathing partially concealed by fur fingerless gloves, steadied her against his back. Deli man plunged harder into the puppy under him and quickly finished his mission. He lay there like a dead man, his hairy sweaty flesh soaking the young woman pinned beneath him. She wriggled to get free, but his weight was too much and she had to endure his smothering folds until he woke up a few minutes later and rolled off. The doggy domme was long gone, cleaning her red prong as she moved about the crowd seeking her next victim.

Benny's hands worked furiously, repeatedly bringing himself to the edge, teasing himself as long as he could stand it. He scouted the multiple screens. The room had turned into a veritable menagerie of limbs, touching, stroking, and entering. Everyone was agreeable and thriving in their ecstatic naked pile.

"What's that?" Benny enlarged screen number two. It was Laguna violently humping into the overstretched mouth of one of the puppy girls. He stood over her and pounded, his expression a rictus of violent lust. The girl was pushing away

107

against his thighs, her arms and legs straining to protect her overstretched jaw muscles. But Victor held her by the back of her head and pounded into her, battering her petite face.

Benny watched, noting the camera and footage number. The screen featured Victor's face and the face of his victim in the same frame. Benny could not have planned it better. Victor's head flew back and his hips bucked spasmodically. The puppy girl gagged. Her eyes teared as she gagged on his suffocating semen.

When he was done, Victor shoved her away and she toppled onto the ground. He shook the excess from his member onto her. He pulled up his pants and wandered into the crowd.

Benny wilted. His hand slowed. He scanned the room again, looking for any morsel that revealed intimacy, real contact. Then he saw it.

Art Croakie watched as a well-hung man banged furiously against the buttocks of the woman before him, kneeling at the edge of a bed. Croakie watched and moved around the couple, touching her and stroking himself. He pinched and rubbed the woman's nipples and in one movement insinuated himself beneath her, his face just below her snatch. Benny saw Croakie nudge the woman's head down and she began to suck him. Croakie's hands flew up and down her back and rested on her ass. He pulled her cheeks wide open as the man pounded deeply into her. Benny could see Croakie's head moving below her, presumably licking her.

Suddenly the man pulled out his glistening member and jerked himself hard. The woman moved forward and the sperm flooded Croakie's face, some of it entering his Lubridone-intoxicated mouth. Croakie laughed good-naturedly, sat up and wiped his face.

"Gotcha," Benny exclaimed, jotting down the location of the scene. He fast-forwarded on and off for the next hour. His prick was now sore, red, and yearning for release. Then he came across another gem.

Victor was eagerly screwing Croakie's statuesque wife Beatrice while Art knelt beside them looking at their intimate connection from every angle and stroking himself. Watching intensely, Croakie timed his orgasm so that it coincided with Victor's, then moved silently away to an abandoned couch.

Benny watched Croakie sitting by himself, his facial expression a rich and complex mask of intimate emotions. Benny loved seeing it. What was that about?

Benny reached for the hand cream so that he could relieve himself and get some sleep. He had been at it for hours and his sore dick needed release. In his exhaustion, he stared at random images of flesh and connection and pounded out a brief, stinging victory. He shut down his monitor and fell asleep. His vigilant cameras continued recording.

CHAPTER 30

The next evening, Benny reviewed the rest of the warehouse recordings, then switched to the camera inside the Camaro. He saw Laguna's dome light flash on, but it was a routine traffic stop. He took off his pants and folded them onto a hanger and saw the light flash on again. He checked the time: Almost midnight. Who is that?

He peered at the screen, making sure of the identities. Beatrice Croakie again. And is that... fur? Is she still in her dog outfit? Hell, yes, she is!

Laguna and Beatrice sat quietly. Victor looked straight ahead, his sweaty face stolid and expressionless. Beatrice, a sensuous battleship of a woman, fleshy and hungry, looked at Victor with imploring eyes.

"Victor, I want to tell you that I love you. I've never felt like this with anyone else in my life. I know that our lives are complicated and mixed up. I know that you have a family and I'm married too. I don't know what to do about it. I just don't know..." Tears streamed down her face. She sobbed into a handkerchief.

Benny saw Laguna's hands twitch as though he was aching to reach out to the sobbing woman beside him, but he kept them at his sides. "I want to help you, baby, but I just don't know how. I don't know what to do. I'm confused. I'd much rather spend my time with you. I hate it at home, except for my little Henry." Victor put his hand over his face and shook his head.

"Let's just go away, Vic. We can take Henry. We can find a place to be together, just us. I can't do this anymore. You're a real man, Vic. I can't stand having him touch me. It's been over for years." Beatrice sobbed louder, her shoulders shaking.

Victor's hands lost the battle. He reached out and pulled her to him, caressing her plump bare shoulders. They sat that way for a while.

Suddenly the door opened. "There you are, I was looking all over for you. We gotta go, Bea, the boys are coming over for a few after-party shots."

Benny watched Croakie's coarse hand pulling Beatrice away from Victor's embrace. She turned to Laguna and mouthed 'I love you.' Once she was out of the car, Croakie leaned back in.

"And you, hombre – if Fawn Fallingsnow doesn't take that tape down, just take care of her for good. We'll talk tomorrow." Croakie offered Victor a manly fist bump.

Croakie and Beatrice left. Benny watched Laguna sitting in the dark, muttering to himself and shaking his head. Then something startled the cop. Laguna rolled down the window, and Bill Dhey poked his face in.

"Come on over to my house tomorrow night, and bring some Lubers. We have a little party scheduled. Different people, some friends of mine from Portland. I want to introduce you to the real Zebra Club. You got more Lubers, right?"

"Sure," said Laguna.

"My place is up in the Coburg Hills." Dhey gave him the address and walked off.

CHAPTER 31

It was early and he could hear his young son watching TV in the living room. Victor Laguna had thought he would be able to sleep late and save some energy for his next late-night ramble.

Then he heard the theme song. This was their time together, cherished time to be on the couch with his son. His wife snored calmly beside him. Victor got up. Henry was on the couch when Victor came in with their bowls of cold cereal. The four-year-old smiled up at his daddy and reached for his bowl: a yellow plastic bowl with red printed boats on it.

Vic gave him the bowl and sat beside him.

It was "BaDoBo," Henry's favorite show. They watched it whenever they could. Vic hated to miss it, even though there had not been a new episode made for two years due to a court battle over the child star's assets.

They knew the lines by heart. Little BaDoBo, the friendly, comical pudgy know-it-all, continually smart-mouthed his friends, his parents, his teachers and anyone else he came into contact with. It was only his pretty little girlfriend neighbor and his dear aunt who know pudgy BaDoBo's heart of gold and inner sensitivity. Victor had come to think of himself as BaDoBo.

"Dios mio," said Mr. Rapona, BaDoBo's teacher. It was a tag line used in the show every day. It cued the laugh track. It was also the moment when Henry would look up into Victor's eyes with a smile. That moment was Victor's redemption, week after week. No matter how much mean-spirited violence Victor had committed the night before, Henry's smile on cue, when Mr. Rapona said "Dios mio," washed it all away.

When the show was over, Victor showered and returned to his ugly world. His teeth were sharpened, his unrepentant lizard-self eager once again for revenge. Every morning, he reloaded his gun with the pain from his childhood. He carried it around with him all day with the safety off.

But today Victor was celebrating a victory. He had been invited to the big dance. Today he was somebody, at least according to Wild Bill Dhey. He was bringing the dope to Bill Dhey's private sex party. He would be turning on the crowd. Nobody else in the entire Willamette Valley, or even the world, had access to Lubridone.

But why can't I get high on the damn things anymore? Victor knew nothing of Malcolm's insight that after the first-use heightened experience, Lubridone became merely great medicine for the joints.

Victor sorted through the closet for just the right clothes. The party started at six. He had the entire day. Let's see, casual or formal? He looked at every item in the closet, then finally chose a dark blue shirt with a black tie. He packed a small bag with a change of clothes for the party and a big baggie of capsules.

CHAPTER 32

Victor's excitement cost him his appetite until about three. He had driven all over Eugene, stopping at parks and stores, nothing quenching his agitation. Eating a sandwich at Brails Restaurant he felt a strong sexual attraction to the waitress. Ah, that's what I need. He paid and left quickly. Across town was a discreetly located adult bookstore.

Inside the curtained front door, Laguna was overwhelmed by the hundreds of slick, smutty covers -- books and magazines and videos. He meandered in a daze, picking up one after another, feeling his penis stir and twitch.

When Victor looked up, the clerk was pulling on a pair of orange rubber gloves and wiping down the counter with bleach solution. . The clerk caught Victor's eye, then glanced a foot or two downward and back up again. He stepped out from behind the counter and came close enough to speak in a low mutter. "You know, a lot of our customers like to go to the last booth, number 8, it's a great place to find some release. It just takes some quarters, or you can pay up front and I can put the movies on a timer for you."

"Yeah, here, give me five dollars' worth." Victor handed him his money, and the clerk pointed an orange finger around the corner.

Once inside the claustrophobic little booth, Victor opened a Luber capsule onto his tongue. He kept the bitter powder in his mouth, mixing it with saliva. He wanted a quick high. Maybe this time I'll get off.

A movie was already playing. There were forty channels, each with a different scenario. The room was small and clean, with paper towels and a wastebasket. There was even a clean chair, but Victor chose to stand. He moved the dial from channel to channel:

Click. The skinny blonde who's been at it since her teenage years bobbed her bleached head up and down on a bearded biker's dick. Her skanky meth-reduced cheeks vacuumed his hard-on. Her skull was visible clearly through her diminished flesh....

Click. The plump housewife was on her hands and knees on the bed, the enormous black man with a tree-trunk-sized erection battered her from behind while she screamed....

Click. Two pretty young women in their late thirties were dressed as schoolgirls, hair in braids, eating each other's pussies, with their pleated parochial school dresses pulled up to their waists....

Click. A beautiful woman was taking her clothes off as her boyfriend watched. Bingo. Victor pulled out his fat dick and began to stroke it, hard. He anxiously yanked, but suddenly somehow the scene on the screen was no longer interesting.

Click. The man moved his loins over her face and plunged his cock deep into her mouth, his knees at her shoulders, her hands rubbing the backs of his thighs.

Where's my high? C'mon Lubers, do your stuff.

Out of the corner of his eye he saw the hole in the wall. A slim hand with painted fingernails motioned him closer. Victor eagerly allowed the hand to caress him. It pulled him through the wall and a supple mouth worked him into frenzy. His thighs pressed tightly against the bleached walls, his pants puddled around his ankles, he humped hard into the wall until he let go. Ah, sweet release.

He heard the sound of throat-clearing. Before he was able to wipe himself, close his pants and get out of the room, he heard footsteps hurrying down the hall and the slam of a door. He had to find her. He had to get her number. It was the best blow job ever.

Victor rushed to the front desk "Did she leave?"

The clerk motioned his head toward the door and Victor ran out.

The clerk turned and spit Listerine into the wastebasket beside him. He slid his delicate painted fingernails back into his orange rubber gloves.

CHAPTER 33

Victor knocked on the door of Bill Dhey's mansion. A woman with a painted cat face opened the door.

She knew who he was. "So where are the pills, big boy? C'mon, let's get this party going, huh?" She pushed his shoulder gently. He took a deep breath. He towered over this petite celebrant.

"The pills, Bill told me to get you and the pills. Did you bring a costume? You're supposed to be dressed. It's required. Never mind. We have extras. How about a donkey suit? No? We have a really sexy weasel."

"I don't wear no costumes." He took the bag of capsules from his travel case.

She looked at him for a long moment, then shrugged. "Whatever. Let's go." She grabbed his hand and pulled him along.

Bill greeted him at the door, wearing a lion pelt over his shoulders. The head of the lion atop his head made him even taller than Victor. Bill had been drinking; his jollity was obvious and exaggerated.

"This is a lot different than the little Zebra Club you have down in town. This is the real Zebra Club. Just relax, Vic, let it happen, my friend. You had a good time yesterday. Uh huh. I saw you. The mayor was sure happy with you banging his wife like that, quite a spectacle." Bill grinned and pounded Victor's back in a good-natured way. He held out a metal dish.

Victor poured most of the capsules out and handed the dish to Bill.

"That was different. He likes to see me with his wife."

"Let me fix you up with a costume. Come on," said Bill.

"I don't wear no costumes. I already told her that."

"Not an option, my friend. We require costumes. Let Lindsay fix you up." Bill turned around and called to a slim woman wearing painted-on snakeskin.

"Fix up our guest with our warthog costume." Bill slapped Victor on the back and walked off.

Who does he think he is? But he let himself be led into a back room, where Lindsay dressed him in a bristly warthog mask and cape. Victor looked at himself in the mirror. Godammed stupidest thing I've ever seen.

Lindsay left and Victor wandered around. He grabbed a drink and found a large pillow in the corner of the room, so he could watch and be alone. He sat brooding, angry and humiliated. He thought about leaving, but felt he had to stay for social reasons that he couldn't define. The first drink started to take effect. The waitress came around and he grabbed another.

The booze made him sleepy and he dozed. He woke up sharply to soft pressure on his groin. A tall blond woman in a feathered bird costume nuzzled her beaky face against his crotch.

"Hey, what the hell!" Victor pulled back from the kneeling woman.

She stood up. "What's wrong with you? Doesn't Mr. Warthog want to join us? Feels like you have a wonderful piece of pork in your pants."

"It's been a tough day. I just want to fall asleep."

"Can I lie down next to you, then?"

"I guess so," Victor said as he cautiously lay back down.

"Now, that's not so bad, is it?" The woman snuggled in next to him and Victor felt comforted. Then he realized that she had taken Lubridone. He could feel her purring. Ah, the joy of first-time Luber intoxication.

"Tell me about these people. Who are they?" Victor asked directly into her ear.

"They're all extremely wealthy folks from Portland. They come down to Eugene to get their kicks and keep their Portland images clean." She turned as she spoke to better point out the attendants. "See that lanky guy with the black eye mask? He's Derek Lo, he owns most of Chinatown. They call him Ek, Ek Lo."

"Who's that fat guy dressed like an ape?"

"He's Hy Chup-eye-chun, he's from I don't know where, someplace foreign, a big realtor. Apartment houses are his thing."

"What about the guy next to the table with the small dark-haired woman?" Victor asked.

"That's Farley DuPriest of the Portland Opera Council. There's Sebastian Orville. There are a lot of opera aficionados here. See that woman with the red hair dressed like a snake? She's Mary Palance, the soprano."

"How do you know all of this stuff?"

"I'm Bill's wife, Doris. Well his second wife, anyhow."

"Dios Mio." The words escaped his mouth without volition, but at the sound, Victor's panic and confusion returned suddenly.

"What did you say?"

"Oh, just something I say sometimes."

"Sounded like 'Dios Mio.' I always hear that in the morning on TV, Elsa our cook watches this show with her little daughter. There's this guy who says that all the time, it's very funny."

"BaDoBo. I know the show." A tear formed as Victor thought about Henry. He didn't want to think about his innocent son in this creepy environment.

"It's OK, Victor. Let me lean against you and you can put your arm around my shoulder. You'll feel better."

Victor did as he was told and it calmed him. Night after night of hard living suddenly caught up with him and he felt a deep exhaustion. He was awakened from his doze by a hand on his thigh, just resting there.

"Man, guy's got a fat dick, huh?"

"Holy shit, I want some of that."

Doris was gone. Kneeling before him was a woman dressed as a clown. She had his thick penis in her hand and was licking it. Against his will he felt aroused. He humped hard into her mouth.

"Not so fast, hon. Let's get some use from this ol' fireplug."

She straddled him and he entered her abruptly. He felt her warm wet grasp. She rocked with increasing rapidity, her head back, uttering loud gasps. Beside her, a woman dressed as a toad knelt and licked at any exposed flesh.

"Hold on, don't let it go," the toad whispered in Victor's. "Save it for me." The toad began to touch Victor's chest. He smelled a foreign perfume. It snapped him from his haze of pleasure.

"What am I doing?" He struggled to get free, dumping the clown unceremoniously on her polka-dotted butt, and pushed the toad to one side. He stood and started to climb into his pants... and a rear takedown sent him sprawling back into the pillows. His pants were pulled out of his hands and the weight of at least three good-sized women was upon him. One straddled his face and rubbed herself over his lips, moaning. Another mounted him. Yet another touched and massaged him all over with her right hand, while using her left to press into the sensitive area behind his balls. At that point, Victor gave up resisting.

The women changed places several times. They flipped him like a rag doll: Victor on top, Victor on his side. Their hands were moving over him, sending him to the brink of release. He couldn't stop thrusting his hips. He was a pumping machine.

A massive woman in a full mask and a Grecian toga was beneath him. A woman was behind him playing with his balls as he slid in and out of yet another woman's dripping sheath. His balls tightened as he readied to empty himself into the woman, whose face was pointed away from him but who seemed oddly familiar. He realized then that this woman's body reminded him of Beatrice's.

Could it be? He thrust harder, thinking about Beatrice, then she gasped his name. The voice was unmistakable. "Vickie, come inside me. I want to feel the hot juice. Harder, make me hurt."

He was nothing if not agreeable. Pounding into her, he let go his confused seed and collapsed, sweat-bathed and sated.

He heard voices and sounds around him and looked up. The group watching his performance surrounded him, nodding and whispering in appreciation.

"Victor, we didn't know you had it in you," Bill Dhey chuckled; the willowy blonde holding his dick nodded in agreement "You're one of us now, Vic, part of the Zebra clan. Come back anytime... as long as you come." Everyone groaned at his stupid drunken joke.

Victor lay there, very confused. He had no social connection with any of these people. The Grecian-outfitted woman had disappeared into the crowd and Victor's discomfort returned, overriding his happy post coital relaxation.

He shook his head forcefully back and forth, clearing away the haze of lust, confusion and old hurt. "So how were things at school today?"

The group, puzzled, looked at each other, hoping that someone would have a clue to this odd verbal puzzle. Victor, though, knew the source of the quote: a scene from BaDoBo he had watched many times with his son. "I know you got into some trouble, there was a note from Mr. Rapona."

The crowd looked at him with smiles. They didn't care what he was actually saying. They were drugged and happy, and plotting how soon they could get him hard again.

"You can't keep behaving like this, my son," rambled Victor. "You're a good boy and you know how to behave in school. Everyone thinks you're funny, and they like you. So why can't you behave?"

The same thought appeared to everyone in the crowd at once: this man isn't going to be good for another fuck for quite a while, maybe not ever. The crowd dispersed in search of a more cooperative centerpiece. Victor continued to quote BaDoBo, whole minutes of it, verbatim and at length, complete with hand gestures; he used a high-pitched voice for BaDoBo and a scratchy Spanish accent for Mr. Rapono.

121

Soon, he was alone on the pillows, nude and sweaty in the half-dark. People wearing costumes surrounded him, merging and separating in a sexual minuet – people he didn't care about.

"Dios Mio."

CHAPTER 34

The light came into the room very early from the giant east-facing windows in Bill Dhey's guest room. Victor had a foul taste in his mouth.. He didn't want to see Bill Dhey, he wanted to be home. He dressed and gathered his stuff. The warthog costume lay in a bristly heap on the floor. He kicked the head as hard as he could, and it bounced off an antique armoire. He found his way downstairs, where his quick getaway was interrupted by Dhey.

"Hey, Victor, great time last night. Leaving soon? No breakfast? No coffee?"

"I gotta get going, Bill, I gotta get downtown pretty quick... uh, thanks for inviting me and putting me up and for everything. I had a great time. So..." Victor put out his hand.

Bill, who was sipping a cup of coffee, shook it. "Hey, Victor, anytime you wanna come up here and party with the big boys, just call me on my cell phone. I'll let you know what's going on. Here's a card." Bill reached onto a shelf behind him and grabbed one. "Oh and – hey, how about more of those Lubers? Can you get some more? They were a big hit."

Victor searched his pocket. He pulled out the baggie. "Here's the last two." He handed them over. "Maybe I can get some more. I'll look around – no promises – they're kind of rare." Victor's eyes shifted toward the door, eager for escape.

Safely in his car, Victor rubbed his face and ran his fingers through his hair. The big engine roared and Victor slowly pulled out of the long driveway. At the wide entry to the street, he looked to his right and saw a familiar white Mercedes parked on the driveway skirt.

Beatrice. Oh fuck. It was Beatrice.

Victor took a deep breath and turned onto the street.

CHAPTER 35

Reverend Ron Hawkins stood before his mirror at the Eugene Hilton, preparing for his press conference. Two older women in Sunday best and big hats sat at a table next to the picture window. They were drinking tea. The heavier of the two women fanned herself.

Ron carefully combed his fabulous thick hair, the outstanding hair that had launched his career. At 14, young Ron had appeared as a hair model in Ebony Magazine. His hair promoted "SpringFro," designed to keep large afros upright under any conditions. They paid him $25 and let him keep the suit, a light green and plum colored leisure number. It was his first taste of publicity and his first chance to wear something stylish, and Ron loved it. Dressed in his suit, he came back to the magazine. He introduced himself to the photographers. He became their gofer, and in return they taught him lighting, sound, cameras, and how to create drama in a photo.

He took all this back to the streets of Harlem, where he started his first church at 17. He relentlessly publicized himself and his achievements and social causes. He began calling himself Reverend Ron Hawkins. What followed were years of media, during which he bombarded the papers with stories, gossip and overblown complaints. He became a well-known agitator, and, while the mainstream press shunned him, he could not be denied.

Hawkins rode his hair to international recognition. As he evolved, it evolved: full afro in his days as a storefront preacher; combed straight up as a civil rights leader; later, during his run for mayor of New York City, he decreased the size, and combed it back a bit.

Now, at 65, he wore important-elder-statesman hair, flecked with gray, slicked back into a wavy pompadour, plastered at the forehead and sticking out at the back like a windswept woodpecker.

The door to the hotel room opened to admit a tall, distinguished black man, dressed in a dark suit with a white shirt. "Brother Ron. The Eugene City Council wants you to call this press conference off. They think they can work this out with you in mediation."

Hawkins turned away from the mirror. "Ron Hawkins won't back down to any punk-assed city council. Brother Deacon, tell them they can mediate my ass."

"Yes, Reverend. You tell 'em," said the heavy woman, nodding her head.

"Amen," said the smaller woman.

"We'll not be shiverin' and glimmerin', while LeBron's quiverin' in his prison cell. Oh no," said Hawkins, shaking his head.

"Oh no. Uh huh. Yeah," the women echoed.

"They be jivin', but Ron Hawkins, he be arrivin' and thrivin.' They try to block me and I will give 'em a shocking."

His hair was perfect. He adjusted his tie in the mirror. "Brother Deacon, who else is with us today?"

"Quite a few, Reverend. We have the local black church here in force, a couple of Portland churches, and an environmental activist group calls itself Greenwerks. They are here in numbers."

"Call that city council. Tell 'em talking time's over. Time to roll over and turn over our man LeBron Booker. This is their last chance, or they can take their song and dance and stick it down their pants."

"Amen," said the ladies.

CHAPTER 36

"Hey, the news is coming on. Quiet!" said the Swede. He tossed a peanut at Nik Omentos, who was talking and gesturing to Big Art Croakie. The three men sat at a table in the back room of Niko's Taverna. They were having their usual Tuesday lunch – spanakopita, ouzo wall-bangers and peanuts.

Swede grabbed the remote and turned up the sound. "… This is Megan Coylie at the Wayne Morse Free Speech Plaza in front of the Eugene courthouse. We're waiting for Reverend Ron Hawkins to make his appearance…" Her voice was nearly drowned by the sound of drums, cowbells and didgeridoos in the background.

"Sounds festive out there, Megan," said the anchorman.

She nodded and beamed cheerfully, holding a hand up to her ear. "I just received word that Reverend Hawkins has arrived."

"Holy shit," said Croakie. "It's really happening." He sat forward in his chair. The camera shifted to a knot of people advancing towards the podium.

"Listen to them drums," said Nik.

"Fuck me," said Croakie.

Swede took a big drink. He chuckled.

"You think this is funny?" snarled Croakie.

"You're in a heap of trouble, boy," said Swede. He tossed a peanut towards Croakie's drink, missed, and picked up his own drink again.

Hawkins was now in front of the camera, pumping up the crowd. He danced a couple of steps, he bobbed, he weaved, and he threw a couple of mock punches. The crowd danced and shouted.

"Fuck me." To Croakie, it seemed like every black person in Oregon was standing behind Hawkins, shoulder to shoulder with the ragged Greenwerks crew.

Hawkins moved to the mike. The crowd quieted. "Brothers and sisters.

For too long, for farrrrr too long, we sat in the back, out of sight, in shame, in disgrace. The reviled, the forgotten, the downnnnntrodden." Hawkins leaned into the microphone, playing the crowd expertly. Brother Deacon held up a poster and the cameras zoomed in: a still shot of Mayor Croakie at his news conference after LeBron's bail hearing – Croakie, two blond kids, and a sad, beat-up LeBron in the upper left corner.

"This is justice?" asked Hawkins.

"Nooooo," said the crowd.

"You call this justice?"

"NOOOO," said the crowd.

"This is a throwback to the dark days of Jim Crow... kie, that's what this is." The crowd yelled its approval. The drums started up.

Hawkins held up his hands. The drums stopped. "It's time to disengage from the gilded age, and step up to the golden age. It's time to free our man, our friend, our precious LeBron Booker, who was wrongfully arrested and molested. It's time to jail the ones who put him there."

"Yeah," shouted the crowd.

"Jail the Croakie!" Hawkins waved his hand back and forth over his head. "Jail the Croakie. Free LeBron!"

The crowd took up the chant. Hawkins looked pleased.

"I'll see all of you at the University of Oregon tomorrow. For the fundraiser!" he shouted. "We're gonna free our man and put the right person in jail. Jail the Croakie... Free LeBron!"

Hawkins stepped away from the microphone and moved into the crowd, handshaking, high-fiving and hugging as he went. The well-dressed black people on the stage were clapping and swaying in time to the chants.

"Jail the Croakie... Free LeBron," shouted the crowd clapping in unison. The drums boomed, people danced. "Jail the Croakie... Free LeBron."

Megan was back on camera. "As you can see, it is very loud here. I can hardly hear myself talk. We're here at the Lane County Courthouse, and big crowds are expected tomorrow at the campus rally. This is not over, it's just the beginning. This is Megan Coylie signing off."

"Thank you, Megan," said the anchorman. "Well, it looks like the mayor is going to have his hands full. And now for our weather –"

Swede turned off the TV.

"Shit," said Croakie. The air in the Taverna was cool, but he was sweating. He dialed his cell phone.

"Who're you calling?" asked Nik.

"I'm calling John Tulley, the godammed district attorney. I gotta get this kid out of jail now. Get this goddammed fucking Hawkins out of town. This cluster-fuck's out of control."

"Jail the Croakie..." sang the Swede softly, clapping and swaying. "Got kind of a nice rhythm to it, don't you think?"

Croakie turned away. Somebody answered his call.

"Hey John, look... Yeah, yeah, I saw it. I saw it. Look, we gotta free this kid, drop the charges, get him out of jail. OK?"

Croakie listened. He frowned. "What? No... Oh come on, John, you can't do that... that's not right. We both run for election. You gotta do this... I'm law and order too... Croakie loves kids..." Croakie let out a big breath. He closed his phone. He looked shrunken.

"So, what'd he say?" said Nik.

"He won't drop the charges. Says he never drops charges if he can make them stick."

"You in a heeeeap of trouble, boy," said the Swede, grinning. He tossed a peanut, and this time it splashed into Croakie's drink. "Goaaaal!" Swede raised his hands over his head.

"Fuck me." Croakie stared off into space.

CHAPTER 37

"Mr. Dhey is here."

"Show him into the conference room, Merry," said Grey Pearce. He was dressed in important-meeting clothes, suit and tie, shoes shined, silver hair carefully combed. "And send in Bugs and Gupta. I may need them."

"Right away, Mr. Pearce."

Pearce sat back and looked at his favorite painting, an original watercolor of racing sailboats rounding a buoy. He wondered what this personal visit from NanoPharm's president was all about. The two men talked at least once a week, emailed more often, and had done so for years. Bill Dhey had no need to visit. But he had called for this 9:00 a.m. meeting at CIRA.

Pearce straightened his tie, grabbed some files, and walked down the hall to the conference room.

Bill Dhey was looking out the window. Pearce noticed that Dhey, dressed in tennis whites, seemed unusually relaxed and casual.

Pearce was an expert on human motivations, moods, emotions, fantasies and attitudes. He'd made an excellent living for many years by combining professional research with gut hunches to fashion entirely new diseases in the public's mind. NanoPharm, the other half of the equation, then supplied the cures, using underperforming existing pharmaceuticals.

Pearce started each project by looking at the legitimate effects of NanoPharm's slower-selling products. He dug into the human psyche and dredged out a suitable primal fear that matched the abilities of the drug. He created advertising strategies to magnify the fear, to spread the fear, to make the fear as viral as a real disease. And with each new fear came with a balm, a happy remedy, in the form of one of NanoPharm's underperforming drugs.

Grey sat down at the conference table. Bugs and Gupta entered the room. Bill Dhey smiled warmly and shook everybody's hand. He seemed unhurried, pleasant, youthful.

What does he want?

"Bill, would you like to hear about our new strategy for NanoPharm's old venereal disease medicine?" Pearce didn't wait for Dhey to respond. "NanoPharm spent a fortune developing Scorpodane, but it was ineffective on any of the rapidly mutating gonorrhea viruses."

"I know. It was my $75 million that got wasted," said Dhey. He turned his palms up, shrugged and smiled: What's $75 million between friends?

"However, it worked to dry out the sinuses of the users. So we re-named Scorpodane. We'll call it Sniffleless and market it for allergy sufferers."

Bill Dhey nodded. "Sure. Sure. Sniffleless is fine. Do it. Good job."

"We have some other new ideas –"

"Not today. I actually want to talk about something else today." Dhey looked at Gupta and Bugs. "Good job, men. I'd like to talk to Grey alone now. Keep up the good work." The two men left.

Dhey took out a baggie containing two capsules, his last Lubers. He put it on the table in front of him. "Could you bring in Malcolm?"

"Sure." Pearce picked up the phone.

A few moments later Pearce heard an almost inaudible tap on the door. In walked Malcolm.

Dhey and Pearce didn't stand up. Malcolm didn't shake hands. He chose a chair in the corner.

"How are you, Malcolm?" said Dhey. His face showed sincere good feeling toward the savant.

"Fine," said Malcolm. He looked up at the ceiling, then glanced out the window.

Dhey handed him the baggie. "Malcolm, could you tell me what this is?"

Malcolm picked out a capsule. He opened the capsule carefully and took a tiny sniff.

His head tilted back. His eyes closed. He had a twitchy smile on his face. He curled his wrists, and put his hands up to his chin. They moved under his chin like the legs of a dreaming dog.

"...Safe, even used every day. Yes, bad stress eats hormones. Release bad stress, and she will get flooded with natural hormones. It softens. It moves energy... pillowy... youthful... not habit-forming... strongly euphoric upon first use..."Malcolm frowned and his hands stopped twitching. "I've...I've...seen...this drug before."

He sat straight up and looked at Dhey for the first time. "Where did you get this?" he asked.

"Uh... never mind. What is it?"

Malcolm didn't answer for a minute. He was staring out the window, his face unreadable. Dhey and Pearce waited.

Malcolm looked at Dhey again. "This is yours."

"What?"

"Two drugs you already own. This capsule is 40% Epithet and 60% Torpidan."

"What?"

Malcolm didn't answer.

Dhey's tapped his pen on the table, thinking. Finally he said to Pearce: "This is a fucking goldmine, Grey. I don't know how this came out of my factory, and got on the street, but this Lubridone" – he held up the baggie – "is revolutionary. It loosens the joints, and relaxes without any narcotic effect. It's a perfect everyday drug for stiff, old, aching joints. And it's a mild aphrodisiac to boot."

Dhey stood. "Stop work on all other new projects. Hire more staff. I want this out in clinical trials ASAP."

"Wow," said Pearce. "Do we have any of this, Malcolm?"

"Uh... yes, one big bottle of each."

"All of it?"

"Yes. Still sealed." Malcolm stood. "I'm leaving now," he said, and walked out.

Dhey watched him go, then turned to Pearce. "We'll make billions."

CHAPTER 38

Malcolm knew Doyle would still be asleep at 9:30 after working the night shift. He knocked on Doyle's door anyway. Nobody answered. He knocked louder. He waited, then knocked even louder.

"Who is it?" said a sleepy voice.

"Open up. Let me in."

Doyle opened the door and Malcolm pushed past him to the living room.

"Where is it?" demanded Malcolm.

"What?"

"The Epithet and Torpidan you were supposed to destroy for me."

Doyle froze. He sat down heavily on the sofa. "Oh."

"Why did you mix up more of Ms. Cup's formula?"

Doyle sighed. "Cup of coffee, Malcolm? Think I'll make some for myself." He went into the kitchen.

"Where are the Torpidan and Epithet?" Malcolm was flushed, his voice tense, his eyes wide open and furious.

"OK, OK, OK." Doyle took a big breath and let it out slowly. "I'm sorry. Look. I really am. I had to do it. I didn't have a choice. My freedom was on the line. I was forced..."

"Give me the rest of it. Now."

"There's none left, Malcolm."

Malcolm looked away for a moment and then turned to Doyle.

"Did you mix up all the Epithet and Torpidan into Ms. Cup's formula?"

"Some."

"What do you mean?"

132

"I made some of Ms. Cup's formula."

"What about the rest?"

"I mixed that up into Blockhead."

"What's that?"

"Blockhead's the street name for the other formula. You know, the formula with the psychotropic qualities you told me about."

"Street name?" Malcolm's eyes narrowed in his thin face. "I trusted you."

"I'm sorry, Malcolm. I didn't have a choice."

Malcolm left without another word.

Doyle watched him go. He had betrayed a lifelong friend, a gentle trusting man, a guy who only wanted to help. Will he forgive me? Maybe not. He watched as Malcolm turned the corner.

CHAPTER 39

Mayor Croakie was leaning back in the beautician's chair, getting a pedicure and avocado-herbal facial. He was dreamily picturing Eugene's current city-hall-of-the-future, with its leaking see-through pond placed directly on top of an underground parking lot. Visit City Hall and get your car washed free! Downtown Eugene was a monument to 1960s urban-renewal vulgarity, plundered by elected Visigoths who had gleefully torn down graceful, historic stone buildings and erected eyesores in their stead.

Croakie's cell phone rang. He sat up a little and pulled a cucumber slice off one eye to check the caller ID. It was his aide, Gareth, calling from Eugene City Hall. He put the cucumber back on his eye and leaned back. "What is it? I said no calls."

"Sorry, sir. We got a situation at the U of O."

"Oh, no." Croakie sat up, cucumber slices falling unheeded to the floor.

"It seems there are about three thousand people there, and most of them are high on some new street drug. Police arrested a student selling the stuff."

The Free LeBron fundraiser was this week's biggest news story, and Croakie was taking the heat. Every night the evening news featured the Greenwerks tape that contradicted Croakie's version of events. Croakie had been bombarded with questions about misrepresenting LeBron's so-called crime. He was accused of criminalizing free speech. When Reverend Ron Hawkins arrived, Croakie became the full-fledged focus of public anger. It was time to strike back. Croakie is tough on crime.

"Call the police chief. I want every officer, on duty and off, in full riot gear, at the university in one hour."

"You may want to think about this a little while first, Mr. Mayor..."

"I said, send the troops in. Dogs, water cannon, the works. I want drug arrests, lots of 'em. Call the TV stations. Get them down there to film it. I'll teach that Hawkins what happens when you mess with Croakie."

Croakie hung up. He lay back in the chair. He took a deep breath. No hurry, plenty of time to enjoy the rest of my facial.

He felt the tide turning.

CHAPTER 40

"Hey sister, good speech. Right on, right on VertBild," said one of the dozens of hippies sitting on the grass.

"Thank you. Thank you," said Fawn Fallingsnow, acknowledging the group with a nod. All eyes were on her. She saw lots of dreamy smiles and hugging.

Fawn picked her way through the crowd of people lounging on blankets and beach chairs at the University, waiting for the Cosmic Bees to start their set. She had just spoken to the crowd about the VertBild housing and neighborhood development concept. Now she was looking for Doyle, who she hadn't seen in days. She'd been ignoring his phone calls, but now, after days of thinking about him, she wanted to clear the air. She wondered if he was even here.

It had been gloomy all day, with a temperature hovering in the high 60s and the sun hidden teasingly behind clouds, but the bright orb suddenly emerged. Fawn stopped, her head tipped back, to soak up the warmth.

The crowd let out an audible sigh, almost as one. Fawn looked around: people were lying hand-in-hand on their backs, leaning into the person next to them, or even cuddling or necking. This is odd.

Fawn saw a barefoot young co-ed walking through the crowd, carrying a tray filled with little paper cups of lemonade. The girl smiled as she passed out cups. "Just one, only one per person," she giggled.

The sun moved back behind its cloud, and the crowd groaned with disappointment, but everyone was still smiling. Many remained lying on the laps and legs of their fellow concertgoers.

A bare-chested college boy wearing a backwards baseball cap came up to Fawn. "Psst! Blockhead, $25 a cap," he whispered. Fawn shook her head no, and the boy moved on. Fawn saw wallets and purses coming out. The boy was doing brisk business.

Blockhead doesn't seem too dangerous.

CHAPTER 41

Benny arrived at the Free LeBron fundraiser just as Fawn Fallingsnow was finishing her speech about VertBild. His typical modus operandi was to sit somewhere on the outskirts of an activity and, from a safe distance, watch. He walked the perimeter searching for a likely spot, and drank a friendly cup of lemonade proffered by a smiling student. "It's more than delicious," she said with a warm grin.

Benny sipped the beverage as he walked and looked. Near the back edge of the crowd, an empty wooden bench called to him. He sat and finished his drink. Wearing sunglasses, Benny could stare at whatever he wished without any issues. He searched for tidbits of intimacy: a gesture, touches, taps, hugs. He found these prizes nestling preciously among the crude, self-serving actions that were more typical of humankind. Within the vast ever-changing buffet before him, these little morsels were always a source of erotic stimulation for him.

Benny found himself relaxing, his senses sharpening. The music was announced and the Cosmic Bees started playing almost immediately. It was as if time skipped ahead on fast forward.

Benny found that he wasn't having to search for the gems of connection he loved; they were all around him in the crowd. Everyone moved to the rhythm of the music. Even if they weren't dancing, it seemed that each action was synchronized to the beat. It made him smile.

Benny had experienced drunkenness, but had found that intoxication made him feel uncomfortably vulnerable. Today was different. He felt full of joy, he felt safe. This was not drunkenness.

A Frisbee came at him from his left. It hit him in the neck and fell onto his lap, followed instantly by a lovely student. In attempting to grab the disk, she had overreached her balance and caught her shin on the edge of the bench. Her full, warm and sweaty body fell into Benny's lap. It was as if he was drowning in her. The smell of her filled his nose; her resinous sharp body odor struck him hard. His hands automatically held her.

Benny had been ten years old, playing a game at a neighbor's birthday party, the last time he held a girl. Her presence in his lap made time slow down. He held her to him and his fingers slid along her soft damp flesh. She was lovely.

He looked down and saw her lively face smiling up at him.

"Thanks for catching me. I think I hurt my foot." She pulled her leg up for him to look at. Instinctively, Benny put his hand tenderly under her bare calf. He saw the abrasion on her lovely tanned shin; he pulled it close to his face and let his fingers trail gently across the ragged mark, his fingers tickling with every fine hair on her leg. He could feel his heart beat in his throat. He patted her as he would a child, in an attempt to make it all better. "Aw," he said.

"Oh, it'll be all right." She slowly moved to get up.

"Don't go," Benny heard himself saying.

"I'll be right here. Come play with us." She reached out her hand and pulled him up. "Here, throw it to that guy." She handed Benny the disk and pointed to a bare-chested guy waving at him.

Benny, against all expectations, threw it perfectly. The disk moved swiftly between four or five players. The injured maiden stayed beside him. She handed him the disk again. This time he looked into her eyes and saw her, her whole self, her caring soul.

She touched him on the shoulder. "Are you all right?"

The question overwhelmed him. Was he all right? He toppled to his knees, breathing harshly. He threw up. He cried. He did both at once, and somehow it felt great.

The girl was kneeling beside him, one warm hand on his back, the other was on his shoulder. She held him close and supported him. The vomiting stopped but the crying didn't. "You're gonna be OK, hon. What's your name?"

"Benny."

"I'm Jamie."

"Benny, this must be new for you. You're gonna be fine." She hugged him and patted him and Benny started to talk. His words came out of him in a gushing torrent.

"It was just too much. I saw every tiny part of you, every skin cell, every, hair, I could smell you, your sweat smelled so wonderful, and when you helped me, when you fell on me it was like Newton's apple hitting me. Life is calling me, telling me to come and play, and all this time, all these years, I've been hiding in my room watching from a distance, holding it away from me. Why, why?" Benny pressed his head against her and sobbed. "I don't want to do this any more. No more."

They held each other and the world swirled around them and they became part of the world. He, Benny, was officially part of the world.

Finally, the storm passed. Jamie got up to play some more. "I'll be right here playing if you need me." She threw the disk.

Benny watched in awe. He felt empty and drained and calm. He sat on the bench and reviewed his life. As each past decision flashed before him, he knew what he had to do to make it right.

He felt immensely grateful for this day, for lemonade, and most of all for Jamie, a perfect stranger, who had appeared at the perfect time and completed his transformation.

CHAPTER 42

Fawn finally saw Doyle. He was standing alone on the stairs of the Erb Memorial Student Union building. He didn't see her. She started stepping over the legs of the sprawled crowd to get to him.

She heard sirens approaching, lots of them.

Doyle saw her. He waved and smiled. That's a good sign.

He stood on the steps and waited for her. They hugged briefly.

"We need to talk," she said.

Doyle didn't answer for a moment. He was still looking out over the crowd. "I was just watching Benny. It was odd. He was actually interacting with people and throwing a Frisbee."

Fawn shivered. "He gives me the creeps. I don't like him."

Doyle shrugged. "He's harmless. I've known him a long time." He nodded his head towards the student union. "Let's go inside."

They found an empty bench. Doyle sat on one end and Fawn at the other, as far away as possible, but facing him.

"Plenty of Blockhead out there," she said.

"Yes."

She took a deep breath. Doyle looked a bit wary.

"I thought I was getting to know you, then this Blockhead business. It makes me wonder who you are."

"What would you like to know?"

"Are you a dealer?"

"No. I'm not."

In the background more sirens were approaching. Then the Cosmic Bees started their second set, drowning out the sirens.

"Then what's going on, Dutch? Tell me the truth."

So he did.

He told her about Laguna busting him in the parking lot a year ago with the planted LSD. When Fawn heard the name Laguna, she froze. Oh my God, he got to Dutch too?

Doyle told her about turning snitch. He told her about the latest shakedown when he had nothing to give Laguna, until Malcolm showed up with the formula for Ms. Cup's arthritis. He told her about mixing up the Lubers. He told her about mixing up the Blockhead.

As they talked, they moved closer to each other on the bench. Then they held hands. When he finished telling her everything, they hugged for a long time. She cried a little, finally releasing some of her fear about Laguna.

She decided she would never tell him about that horrible night when Laguna had showed up at her house.

They sat together quietly for a while, just holding hands, until Fawn broke the silence between them. "You know, from what I can see, Blockhead doesn't look extreme. People are hugging and talking and peaceful. I don't think it's bad. Maybe I'd even try it someday."

"How about now?" Doyle reached in his shirt pocket. He pulled out two capsules. "I haven't taken any since that first and only time. I was hoping we could take Blockhead together."

"Why not?" She held out her hand.

CHAPTER 43

"In New York City, we have our own money-grubbing billionaire problem," thundered Reverend Hawkins over the loudspeaker. "We have the Goldman Sachs billionaires. We have the hedge fund billionaires. We have the banker billionaires. And... we have... The Donald."

The crowd was standing, enjoying it. Several beach balls were floating overhead. Each time someone hit the ball, the crowd nearby said "Ahhh."

Behind Hawkins stood members of Oregon's black community, interspersed with Greenwerks members. Hawkins had a clear view of distant rows of riot police behind the crowd, geared up and ready.

"Yeah, we have The Donald, and the Lord knows that's bad enough. But you here in Eugene – you have...The Croakie!" The crowd roared with laughter.

"The Croakie, he don't give up, even when he's wrong. Look behind you, everybody." As one, the crowd turned. The police advanced a few steps.

"The Croakie has his cops. You good people are peacefully assembled, helping your friend, our brother LeBron Booker. The Croakie, and the Croakie Cops, they are itching to start hackin' and crackin' and whackin' and ransackin', and all we're doing here is a little yakkin'. Am I right?"

The crowd roared.

"They want to take you, they want to shake you. For what?"

A Greenwerks man walked up to Hawkins and whispered something in his ear. Hawkins beamed.

"I just heard the most wonderful news, brothers and sisters. We have raised a total of $32,000 for the bail and legal defense of our brother LeBron!" Hawkins looked to the sky and held his hands up. "It'll be soon, brother LeBron, and you will be returned to your loved ones. Free LeBron! Jail the Croakie! Free LeBron! Jail the Croakie!"

The emcee walked onto the stage. "Up next," he read from a card, "is Eugene's own Brazilian samba marching band, Samba Ja!" The crowd yelled its welcome. More dancing!

Hawkins waved and danced and threw a combination of punches as he left the stage. Backstage, a barefoot girl carrying a tray with small paper cups passed by sweaty, dry-throated Hawkins.

"I'm mighty thirsty, sister," he said, taking a cup and draining it in one swallow. "Delicious! May I have another?"

"No sir," the girl giggled as she pulled the tray away from his hand. "Only one per person."

CHAPTER 44

Croakie sat in the police command van.

"Take 'em. Get those drugs. Arrest anyone holding," he said into the two-way radio.

The police started banging their shields with their nightsticks. They advanced slowly.

The crowd turned as a group and faced the police, quiet and motionless. The police moved step by step forward.

The crowd stayed where they were.

The police stepped forward some more. Then, in a heartbeat, the crowd broke and started fleeing in every direction except towards the police.

"Hold on a second," said Croakie. The police stopped.

In less than a minute almost all of the three thousand people were gone. The KLCC radio broadcast booth was empty. The stage was empty.

"Shall we pursue?" the police captain asked Croakie.

"Not yet. Let's keep together. Maybe this is over," said Croakie. He saw his opportunity to turn the tables on the protesters slipping away. The campus was as empty and quiet as Christmas vacation. "I guess we should stand down."

The captain didn't answer. He had his hand to his head, listening to his radio ear bud. The captain was shaking his head in disbelief. "The entire crowd just reassembled a couple blocks away, down on Agate Street by Hayward Field. Traffic is stopped in both directions."

"What?" Croakie heard the drums of Samba Ja start up from the direction of Hayward Field.

"March on them! Now!" shouted Croakie into the radio.

CHAPTER 45

Doyle and Fawn held hands and danced with thousands of others in Agate Street. Exhilarated and clear-headed, Fawn felt connected to every one of them. Across the crowd, she saw Benny dancing wildly.

Everyone danced. Ron Hawkins and his entourage were dancing next to the Samba Ja drummers.

Suddenly, the drums stopped. The crowd turned. The line of police was advancing slowly towards them.

The crowd tightened ranks. Fawn and Doyle joined in. They swayed together and held hands. Then everyone's nerve broke simultaneously and the crowd scattered, once again fleeing in every direction except toward the police.

By the time the row of officers arrived on Agate Street, only a few were left, shuffling about on the sidewalks, hardly a menace to society.

Fawn and Doyle took a side street and made their way east and south. Others were also making their way in the same direction. Without exchanging words with anyone, they all knew the crowd's new destination – Washburn Park.

Back in the command van, Croakie was perplexed.

"What do we do?" asked the captain.

Croakie scratched his head. He took off his headset, and walked to the door.

"Call it off. Send the troops home. If they assemble again, watch from a distance."

Croakie threw the headset on the table. "Fuck it."

CHAPTER 46

Two days later, Benny was cleaning out his room. Black plastic bags of hoarded old clothing were piled in the corners, ready to go to the thrift store; he'd kept only a few things that were in good shape and that he really liked. He carried the bags out to the front porch. As he came back into the house, his mother was sitting in her usual place in front of the TV.

"Mom, I'm planning on moving out. I'm finally gonna do it."

"Benny," she said, looking up at him from her big chair, "anytime you want to come back for dinner, you let me know and I'll make you something special." She smiled and turned back to the tube.

"I'm sorry I've been such a burden to you all these years. I just didn't realize it." He touched her shoulder and went upstairs to his room.

Back in his room, Benny scanned the recordings from what he'd come to think of as his Camaro-Cam. He paused the playback when Laguna appeared on the monitor. The cop was forcefully pushing the head of a crack whore down onto his penis. His face was twisted in a cruel grimace.

Benny recognized this particular victim. He had seen her once before on the tapes. He called her "Lamb-chop" because the sounds she made while fellating Victor reminded him of someone eating flesh from a greasy bone. "I think Victor needs see this lovely picture."

After printing out a copy of the photo, Benny went to the GPS tracker. Victor was not far. Benny set an alarm so that his cell phone would buzz when Victor got home for the night, and got back to work cleaning his room.

The buzzer sounded at 10 p.m. Benny put on thin rubber gloves. He wrote out a note on a clean piece of paper, put it into an envelope with the photo, and continued to clean his room. A half hour later, Benny strolled through the dark neighborhood and walked up to Victor's Camaro. He slid the envelope through the slightly opened window so that it landed on the driver's seat.

"It's all over, Victor." As Benny strolled home, he called Jamie on his cell. "Want to help me find an apartment?"

"Sure, Benny. Why don't you get a paper and come by? We can look together."

CHAPTER 47

For two days Victor had been on edge. He couldn't concentrate on his job and drove aimlessly around town all day. He jumped on every incoming call as soon as it rang.

He was pulling out of a convenience store, after receiving his usual free cappuccino, when his cell phone buzzed. As he grabbed for it, his adrenaline-fueled clumsiness tipped a large quantity of hot foamy milk onto his lap. He tossed the entire cup out the window into the parking lot, swearing, and put the phone to his ear.

Benny's voice went through a state of the art voice disguiser that made him sound like a caricature of a German film director, complete with arrogant swagger and slight accent. He was calling, of course, from a cheap disposable cell phone.

"You know vy I am calling you, don't you, Victor?" the voice said.

"Who is this? I find out who this is and I'm gonna wring your neck."

"No need to get angry. You must learn to obey. If you do as you are told, no one vill see the picture."

"OK, so you got me, she's just a whore. Big deal. Whattya want from me?"

"You don't vant to lose your job, do you, Victor? So vy don't you think about behaving? You're a public servant, so serve. You don't vant your boy to learn about what his father does during the day, do you, Victor?"

"Leave him out of this." Victor's knuckles were white where he gripped the phone.

"I vill leave you alone ven our business iss complete."

"Whattya want me to do? Let's get it done."

"Not yet. Await further messages. I vill be in touch."

"Who is this? When I find out, I'm…"

Benny hung up.

Two days later, Benny printed out several more photos and a note: YOU WILL HEAR FROM ME SOON. At two a.m. he slid the envelope through Laguna's car window.

Comfortably ensconced at the desk which now stood in a near-empty room, he watched Laguna leap for the phone like a drowning man trying to grab a rope. He hung up. He set an alarm to remind him to do this every two hours for the next several days.

Laguna sat in his Camaro and stared at the photos of himself with Lamb-chop. As he cruised during the day, he peered suspiciously at the buildings he passed, hoping to catch a glimpse of a telephoto lens poking out of an upper-story window.

OK, I've let him simmer long enough; he's ready now. "Will you obey me?" Benny asked him, knowing that "Vill you obey me?" was coming out the line in a voice an octave deeper than Benny's rather nasal tenor.

"Whattya want me to do? Just tell me already. Enough."

"I say ven you have had enough! Not you, Victor. Is that clear, or do you need to think about it for another veek or so?"

Benny, enjoying himself, switched to the "coarse whisper" setting. "You vill receive several more photos in the next day or so. I vill put them on your back porch. You vill be there on your porch, wearing a blindfold, or I vill not drop them off for you. Do you understand?"

"OK, I'll be there. When?"

"I will not tell you ven. You must be there with your blindfold on from tonight until they are delivered."

"Are you fucking kidding me? I'm not hanging out on my back porch with a blindfold on all fuckin' night!"

"Do you need another lesson, Victor? Do you vant to make front page news tomorrow?"

Benny heard a ragged sigh of defeat coming out of the phone. "OK, OK. I'll be there."

150

"If I don't see you there, you von't get the directions, and I vill call you every day. Do you want that, Victor?"

"No, OK, I'll do it. I'll put on a blindfold and sit on my back porch. I'll be there. Just let's get this over with."

"Do not rush me, Victor. Just be there."

Benny hung up, giggling, imagining Victor sitting blindfolded on his back porch all night. The next morning, he walked by and peeked into Victor's yard to see him sitting in a chair with a black blindfold on; the reality was even better than his imagination. That night Benny dropped a set of instructions and photos into the narrow opening in Victor's car window.

After breakfast the next morning, Benny called Victor. "Victor, you have behaved yourself. The photos are in your car, along with instructions."

"What do you want me to do?"

"Read the instructions and follow them." Benny hung up.

CHAPTER 48

Mayor Croakie picked up one of the photos Laguna had just thrown on his desk. "Pretty good shot."

Laguna pulled up his shirt lapels. "I guess so, if you want to see your mayor fucking someone dressed like a leopard." He jutted his chin out and moved closer to the mayor's face.

"I thought we were in this together, Victor," Croakie said nervously.

"Not today, pal. And if you don't do what I say, this picture's goin' public, you unnerstand?" Victor's face was now nearly touching Croakie's.

"Bastard! How could you do this to me?" Croakie hissed. He stood, his tall lean frame looming over Victor's squat sturdy one.

Victor squared his shoulders and stayed put. "I call the shots now, Art. There's plenty more photos just like this and worse. You lay a hand on me and this shit hits the front pages."

Croakie glared. His pursed lips tightened angrily. The two men locked eyes for a long, tense moment, but Croakie gave first. He sat down stiffly. "Whattya want, Victor?"

"You need to end the LeBron trial, get him out of jail ASAP. It's over."

"OK," Croakie said quietly.

"You have to approve support for the VertBild proposals."

"So now you're an eco-friendly guy… with a Camaro?"

"Just do it, Art." Victor breathed into Croakie's face, his yellow teeth within biting distance.

"Okay." Croakie shook his head.

"Give me an apartment in one of your buildings. There's a woman I need to meet privately."

152

"This is extortion, Laguna. I thought we were friends." Croakie's words steamed out of his mouth in a low growl.

"You got plenty of apartments. I want a nice one, too. Something near Amazon Park." Victor turned his head at an angle as he spoke, like a bird getting ready to grab a worm.

"Bastard."

"And one more thing. I get to ride shotgun. Whenever you take your boys out, I get a call and you pick me up."

Croakie nodded.

"Any one of these things don't happen and your fat ass is in the news, you unnerstan?"

"Yes. I unnerstan."

CHAPTER 49

Benny's bedroom in his Mother's house was jammed with cardboard boxes. A U-Haul sat in the driveway. Benny stood amidst the clutter, his laptop open atop a stack of boxes. Just a couple more things to do.

He booted up "Email Interceptor" and plugged in Victor Laguna's full name and address. The program searched the web, located Laguna's personal computer, and logged Benny into it. Benny typed in a series of commands and hid them in Laguna's computer. If anybody looked in Laguna's computer, any evidence of intrusion would only appear on the screen in writing that was the exact color of any background on the screen: high-tech invisible ink. He encrypted his files with unbreakable hacker encryption, so that any attempt to copy his command files would freeze the computer, requiring it to be restarted. When the computer restarted, the command files would be erased. That should do it.

Benny copied all the footage from Laguna's Camaro and uploaded it onto Laguna's computer in hidden files. He installed a remote activation command, allowing him to move the files to Laguna's desktop later on. At that point, anyone looking at the desktop would see the files listed there.

Benny copied all the Zebra Club sex footage and uploaded it. He also uploaded internet-ready, edited video clips made from the juiciest moments.

From Laguna's email program, Benny sent the edited clips of forced blowjobs and Zebra Club hijinks to YouTube and to porn sites worldwide. He signed Laguna's name to all of them.

Next, he uploaded a PayPal receipt for all the spy equipment installed in Laguna's Camaro, and created a link that would stream all future Camaro-Cam footage directly to Laguna's computer. It was now clear that Laguna had bought the Camaro's bugging devices for the purpose of taping himself having sex on duty or at group sex parties.

He uploaded edited versions of the audio files of Croakie ordering Laguna to threaten and neutralize Fawn. He uploaded the video clip of Laguna threatening Fawn in his car, and forcing Fawn to touch his penis. He uploaded Croakie laughing when Laguna reported back.

From his own computer, Benny created a temporary Hotmail account using an alias and "Hide Me" software. From this account, Benny emailed the worst of the Laguna and Croakie tapes to the district attorney, to the Eugene police, to the TV stations, to The Eugene Weekly, and to sites all over the Internet. You're a porn star now, Laguna.

He exited Laguna's computer and destroyed all traces of the connection.

Benny checked the time. Jamie would be here soon to help him move to his new rental house in the University district.

Last night Benny had put all his spy cameras, bugging and tracking devices and other suspicious hardware in a burlap sack. He had driven his car back and forth over the sack several times, then disposed of the crushed contents into several dumpsters around town. He was now camera-less for the first time since childhood.

I've got one last thing to do.

But Benny didn't want to do it. He had put off doing it.

He gritted his teeth. It's now or never.

He looked at his computer screen. He took a deep breath. For a long moment, he couldn't bring himself to do anything. Then he shook his head forcefully. He thought of Jamie.

Hardly believing what he was doing, he moved his cursor and pulled up the main file containing all his surveillance tapes and photos, all his pictures. Everything. Every image, every tape, every picture going back to childhood and the first pictures he had ever taken.

One last look...

He scrolled through the folders, looking at the names and dates on the folders. He remembered each picture, each thrill, each secret pleasure.

One particular file stopped him.

He opened the folder. He copied one picture and printed out a high-quality 3X5, then closed all the files.

Only his desktop was open. He inserted a flash drive.

He pressed "enter," and the flash drive wiped his computer clean forever.

He had already destroyed the backups. Out of a lifetime of picture-taking, only one photograph remained. He put the 3x5 into a small envelope and dropped it into his shirt pocket.

The doorbell. It was Jamie. Time to load the truck.

He turned off the cleaned computer and put it into a box of stuff to be donated to charity.

CHAPTER 50

Laguna waited in front of his house. The large black car pulled up and Laguna slipped into the shotgun seat as promised.

"Hey, guys, how is everybody?" said Victor uneasily, feeling out his new position.

"Just great, Victor," said the Swede, whose height forced him to crunch into the backseat by sliding his ass forward and leaning back uncomfortably. His hostility towards Victor was unconcealed. "How about some peanuts?"

"Sure," said Victor.

The Swede grabbed a handful and threw them at Victor, showering him.

"Hey, these are my good clothes, clown boy. You want me to pull you out of the car and rub your face in dog shit?" Victor turned in his seat, his hand in a fist.

Nik put his hands up. "Hold it, hold it. We gotta have peace if we're gonna have some fun, guys." He turned to the Swede. "Look, I sit in the back all the time, no big deal. Get used to it."

"And you, Laguna," Nik continued. "You got shotgun. That's an important spot. You gotta live up to it. Behave yourself."

Victor turned his fuming face to the front and sulked. After a few blocks he let it go.

"Here, Victor." He turned. The Swede was holding the tall peanut bag toward him. Victor reached in and grabbed some of the peace offering. "Thanks, Swede." He turned forward, cracked the shells and ate a few.

"We having fun yet?" shouted Croakie. Nobody responded. "We having fun yet, you fuckers?" he repeated.

"Where we goin', Art?" asked Nik.

157

"Oh, you'll see." Croakie guided the long black car into a bumpy alley parallel to Sixth Avenue. Victor knew this area as a heroin dealer's paradise. It was a place where lost souls found desperate relief, where Mexican immigrants escaped from financial oppression only to find homelessness and destitution. It was where runaways of all ages, unable to cope with a hyperactive over-demanding jigsaw puzzle world, lay along the roadside like used fast-food bags, embedded permanently into the lush green landscape of Eugene.

This was blow-job country, where he had found and coerced countless poor souls into his Camaro and down onto his juice-can penis. Victor looked at Croakie as the car lurched over bumps and into ditches.

"Let's have some fun, Vic. Why don't you show us how?" Croakie said. He smiled sweetly at Victor.

"Let's just go get a drink," Vic said. He was squirming in his seat.

"You know the ropes, Vic. Give us a demo," Croakie demanded.

"It's too early to do this, nobody's out yet."

"I think I see someone up ahead."

"That's just some guy with a sleeping bag."

"What are we doin' here?" asked Nik.

"You'll see," Croakie replied. "Won't he, Vic?"

"Knock it off, Art. Some other time. C'mon let's get out of here. I can't do this today."

"Why, 'cause you got your new clothes on?" Croakie taunted.

There was a brief silence. "All this time I thought we were friends. But that's not true, is it?" said Victor.

Croakie turned off the ignition. "How could you think we were friends?"

Victor thought of all they had shared, especially Beatrice. Then he knew. "You're jealous, that's it. You're jealous and angry at me."

"Jealous... of you? Hah. That'll be the day."

"Cut it out." Nik intervened nervously. "What are we doing here in this alley, anyhow? Let's go to some joint, like Vic said. Let's go get a beer and quit the fuckin' arguing."

The Swede said nothing. He looked out the window watching the human scenery: huddled homeless junkies nearly invisible against the trees and garages.

"Jeez, look at her," Nik yelped, pointing out a smudged hippie girl traipsing along with a dog on a rope. "She's gotta be lost. She's just a school kid."

"It doesn't matter to Victor. Isn't that right?" Croakie taunted, looking at Victor.

Victor turned away and seethed.

"C'mon, Croakie, you sick fuck. There's nothing going on here. Let's go get a lap dance or something," the Swede said in his deep resonant voice.

Croakie started the car. He turned right at the end of the alley and pointed the car toward the nearest strip club. A state police car appeared behind him. After a few blocks, the statie flashed his lights. Croakie changed lanes, assuming that the cop wanted to pass. The statie moved behind him and blipped his siren. Croakie pulled over. No one spoke. Nik ate peanuts nervously.

"What seems to be the problem, officer?" The mayor leaned out the window, smiling his billboard-ready smile

"Art Croakie? Victor Laguna?"

"Yes," they said in unison.

"Please step out of the car. I have warrants for your arrest."

"There must be some mistake, officer, we..."

"Out, sir."

Reluctantly, Croakie and Laguna stepped out of the car. They were handcuffed, put into the police car, and driven away.

Nik and the Swede watched the police car recede. "What the fuck was that about?" said the Swede. He got into the driver's seat and started the car. "C'mon, Nik, let's go get that drink."

CHAPTER 51

SIX MONTHS LATER

Jamie was against Benny buying a Camaro, and she didn't understand why he wanted one. It made no sense. Why trade in a Toyota for a gas guzzler?

But Benny insisted. So, on a misty day in November, she drove him down Franklin Boulevard and across the Willamette River to Springfield in her Prius.

Benny had not told her the truth about his life of spying and recording. Every time he thought he was ready, he hesitated. He didn't know how to tell her just a little bit, and he didn't know how to keep her from asking further questions and finding out too much.

He wanted to believe he had changed his life and rid himself of his obsession. He wanted to believe he was in control. He wanted his secret past behind him. But he knew he had to keep some of his secrets forever.

"There it is." Benny pointed to a small, neatly maintained house on a street of blue-collar homes.

Jamie parked the car. She started to get out.

"Wait a minute."

She sat back down. He took a deep breath and made a decision. A group of kids walked by the car carrying a football.

"There's something about this Camaro that I didn't tell you."

She looked at him. She waited.

"It belongs to a guy I've known since grade school."

"A friend of yours, OK..."

"No. Not really a friend. Actually... I didn't like him... I've never liked him... and he didn't like me. He wasn't a friend. But we knew each other, like, at school, at the Nexus."

"And you admire his car, this shiny, red, eight-miles-per-gallon gas hog."

Benny felt his control of the narrative slipping away. "I'm sorry. I'm confusing you."

"Yeah."

"The guy who owns it, Victor Laguna, he's in prison now. I want to help his family. I wouldn't normally buy a Camaro."

Benny studied Jamie's face. He saw she was processing. "Oh." She nodded. "That Victor Laguna, the crooked cop."

"Yeah, that guy. He got three years in prison. The district attorney could have had him for ten, but Victor's lawyer arranged a plea bargain in exchange for his testimony against Mayor Croakie, who's now doing five."

"I know. I read the papers. Good riddance. But that's very thoughtful of you to want to help."

Benny saw most of her skepticism and doubt melt away. Whew.

They got out of the car and pulled their raincoat hoods up. They walked by a house with a chain link fence around the entire front yard. A Doberman scrambled off the porch towards them, barking and wagging his stump of a tail at the same time. They ignored him and he dashed back to his dog bed, his job successfully completed.

Benny rang the doorbell, and a chubby little boy peered through the crack made by the security chain. His mother looked through the crack a moment later.

"Hi, Marta? I'm Benny. I called about the Camaro. We spoke yesterday. This is Jamie."

The woman closed the door and unlatched the chain.

Benny saw that Marta was a thin, athletic-looking brunette, a woman who would be attractive if only she smiled.

She let them in. The boy stayed by her side and gazed up at the strangers.

Marta looked at her child. "Shake hands, Henry."

Benny and Jamie bent over and shook his little hand. The boy moved shyly behind his mother. "I knew your dad," Benny told him. "Victor and I went to school together."

Marta stared at Benny with a questioning, distrustful look. He could see that anyone associated with Victor was tainted in her eyes. The child held his mother's hand.

A long awkward moment passed. Nobody spoke.

"Never mind." Marta waved a hand back and forth. "It's not your fault." She patted her son's head.

Benny pulled an envelope out of his pocket.

"I have something for Henry. Can I give it to him?"

"What is it?"

Benny took a photograph out of the envelope and held it so Marta and Jamie and Henry could see it. "I took this picture a long time ago. This is your father when he was fourteen years old."

Henry took one look at the photo. He dropped his mother's hand and ran into a room down the hall. He didn't close the door.

Marta's sad eyes followed her son. In her eyes, Benny saw a tired, scorned woman, humiliated in public, now desperate, living with a troubled son, with no money, and at the end of her rope.

"He's really broken up," said Marta. "Henry can't understand why his father isn't here. I've tried to explain, but he's furious at Victor for leaving. He feels so abandoned. They were inseparable. What a thing to do to a kid. It just makes you sick."

Benny felt a jolt of regret: I caused this.

Marta held out her hand. "Can I see that picture?" She studied it. "Who are these other people? Friends of Victor's?"

"Ummm... no. More like friends of mine. That boy standing across from Victor? That's Doyle. He just got married two weeks ago." Benny didn't mention that the picture was taken with a secret lunchbox camera, just seconds before Doyle punched out Victor for bullying Malcolm. "See that boy sitting on the bench next to Doyle? That's Malcolm. He was the best man at Doyle's wedding."

Jamie opened her cell phone. She pulled up a picture and held it out for Marta to see. "Here's Doyle two weeks ago, standing at his wedding reception next to his bride Fawn, Malcolm, and me. Doyle's song is on the radio all over the place: 'This Bright Morning'. You probably heard it. "

Benny looked at the photo again. "Malcolm's kind of a genius; he creates medicine. He spends most of his time taking care of his ailing mom and her friend, his grade school teacher. His boss lets him work from home these days. He built a lab for Malcolm in his basement so he can be there as much as he can."

Marta seemed to relax. She handed back the cell phone and put the old photo on the table. "Maybe later on Henry will want to see this. Thank you. I'll hold on to it. That was very thoughtful of you."

"I really do want to buy the Camaro, if it's still available. I have cash," said Benny.

"And I need to sell it. I don't know what I'm going to do. I just barely paid the mortgage last month."

Benny counted out the money on a coffee table while Marta signed the title and the bill of sale. She handed Benny the keys.

"The car needs gas. And the interior got torn up when the cops took the upholstery apart after Victor's arrest, looking for cameras. But it runs fine."

Benny and Jamie shook Marta's hand. "If there's anything else I can do to help, let me know. I mean it," said Benny.

"Thank you." Marta's looked relieved.

Henry came out of the other room. He stood by his mother. In a hesitant voice, he said to Benny, "Can you come over and watch BaDoBo with me?" Marta smiled.

Jamie struck a pose in front of Henry, her hands on her hips, an exasperated expression on her face. "Oh, BaDoBo! Dios Mio!"

Henry's face lit up. "You know Mr. Rapona!"

"Mr. Rapona is my favorite," said Jamie. "My niece and nephew just love BaDoBo."

"If it's OK with your mother, we can come by," said Benny.

"Sure," said Marta. But the look on her face said: Talk is cheap, pal. Let's see if you actually follow through on it.

Outside, Benny got in his new car. The interior was a mess. He turned the key and the engine started immediately with a low, throbbing rumble. He backed into the quiet street. He pressed the accelerator to hear the engine roar.

He looked over at the house, and made a promise.

I am watching over you.

Jurgen "Jug" Brown was born in Bingle Springs, in the outback of Australia, in 1951. His father abandoned his pregnant girlfriend before Jug was born, and his mother died in childbirth. He was raised by aboriginals and missionaries and educated in a one-room Christian school. At 16, he left Bingle Springs barefoot and hitchhiked to Perth. He talked himself onto a ship, and worked as a merchant marine seaman and 2nd mate for the next 15 years travelling the world. He married a Turkish woman, and by correspondence course he received a rare double Masters in Ethnology and Animal Husbandry. Jug Brown has lived in Brisbane, San Francisco, Amsterdam, Paris, Mexico, Glascow, London and Myanmar. He currently lives on the Oregon Coast. His first attempt at writing, *Bush Bash to Drongo 9*, currently out of print, was a sci-fi version of a classic Somerset Maugham book. You can reach Jug at jugbrown@gmail.com.